W0043171

PENGUIN BOOKS

BIG MISTAKE: AN ANTHOLOGY ON
GROWING UP AND OTHER TOUGH STUFF

BIG MISTAKE

An Anthology on Growing Up and Other Tough Stuff

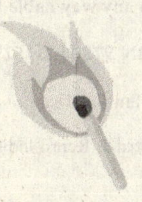

Foreword by SHAHEEN BHATT

PENGUIN BOOKS

An imprint of Penguin Random House

PENGUIN BOOKS

USA | Canada | UK | Ireland | Australia
New Zealand | India | South Africa | China | Singapore

Penguin Books is part of the Penguin Random House group of companies
whose addresses can be found at global.penguinrandomhouse.com

Published by Penguin Random House India Pvt. Ltd
4th Floor, Capital Tower 1, MG Road,
Gurugram 122 002, Haryana, India

Penguin
Random House
India

First published in Penguin Books by Penguin Random House India 2021

Anthology copyright © Penguin Random House India 2021
Copyright for individual stories vests with the authors
Photograph copyright on page 131 © Japleen Pasricha for Feminism in India (FII)

All rights reserved

10 9 8 7 6 5 4 3 2

The views and opinions expressed in this book are the authors' own and the
facts are as reported by them which have been verified to the extent possible
as on the date of publication by the author to the publishers of the book,
and the publishers are not in any way liable for their accuracy or veracity.

ISBN 9780143452973

Typeset in Amiri by Manipal Technologies Limited, Manipal

Printed at Repro India Ltd.

This book is sold subject to the condition that it shall not, by way of trade
or otherwise, be lent, resold, hired out, or otherwise circulated without the
publisher's prior consent in any form of binding or cover other than that in
which it is published and without a similar condition including this condition
being imposed on the subsequent purchaser.

www.penguin.co.in

MIX
Paper from
responsible sources
FSC® C047271

This is a legitimate digitally printed version of the book and therefore might not
have certain extra finishing on the cover.

Contents

A Collector of Scars

Foreword by Shaheen Bhatt

I'm a collector of scars.

I dabble in them as some would stamps, coins, the 'normaler' things.

They were unwelcomed at first, dreadful things.

The wounds would cause deep, throbbing pain where deep throbbing pain should never be.

But they were supplied with such keen interest— I mistook them for adornments worth having.

Most were collected in the twilight years of adolescence.

Apparently, a time when everything is fair game.

A time when the mere hint of dissimilarity is easily weaponized.

Some were supplied by others my age, some by adults who should have known better, some by the very world we live in.

They started off slight and diminutive.

Gradually they grew, they hardened, they set.

They disguised my skin, over time I forgot what it used to looked like.

I thought it was armour, I was wrong. It was a vault.

Nothing in, nothing out.

A fine way to live. Until it isn't.

That's when you go to work.

You try to locate the source of the now dull throbbing that still lives somewhere beneath miles of hardened skin.

You toil only to finally recall you weren't always built this way.

You find you've been altered.

Clumsily cracked open and then expertly sealed shut.

Swathed in defences you didn't know you were capable of fashioning.

Defences that took over and manoeuvred you like a marionette.

You begin the slow, laborious process of chipping away at those outer layers.

Bit by bit, parts of you come back.

Some, you realize, are gone forever, now you work to replace them with something else. Something good.

You wonder how much time was wasted in this doing and undoing and who was lost along the way.

There is a reason suicide is frighteningly common in adolescents.

It's a time of developmental turmoil like no other.

In India alone, the numbers are staggering.

One student commits suicide every hour and 50 per cent of all suicides occur within the 15–29 age group.

It should be unsurprising to learn then, that adolescence is one of the most complex transitions we experience in our lifetime.

It's a time of fast-tracked growth and change, second only to infancy.

The biological, behavioural and social changes make it a time of self-discovery and our experiences during this formative phase can shape the course of our whole life.

The scars you acquire here are the ones that tend to stick, the ones that take the most work to undo.

This, I know from experience.

Mine came from a variety of different things, some worse than others.

Some were survivable, others I'm still learning to survive.

And while my scars are scars—while they're every bit as valid, every bit as painfully acquired as those of others, they came from familiar places and they made familiar shapes.

You see scars like mine every day—if you look carefully enough.

But there are some shapes we don't see as frequently or at all.

Maybe because we've been told to avert our eyes, or been told that they're ugly, or we've simply not been told because they remind us of the truths we prefer to keep hidden.

The stories that fill these pages come in all shapes.

They're the stories we don't hear often enough but perhaps the ones we need to the most.

They're stories about diversity and uniqueness—about glorious uncommonness.

Stories of violence and discrimination.

Stories of how distinctiveness often leaves marks, though it shouldn't.

Stories of queerness, love, body image, friendship, war, feminism, disability and so much else.

These accounts might help someone reading feel seen and understood for the first time in their life.

They might help someone pause to consider those around them more acutely.

They might help you rethink a flippant remark, a casual oversight.

Above all, this powerful collection of stories is a potent reminder that we are not the scars we collect in youth.

And that the more we tell vital stories like these, the fewer scars we will ultimately collect because we will raise a generation inured to contrast and fluent in the art of inclusion.

It is in shining a spotlight on dissimilarity that *Big Mistake* gives us the greatest gift of all, it makes it beautifully mundane.

Shaheen Bhatt
April 2021

Big Mistake

Parvati Sharma

Not all teachers are so bad. We had this one—young fellow—he was supposed to teach us history, but he would keep talking about other things, asking questions without reason. 'Is Instagram a historical record?', 'Can the present change the past?'—things like that. The semi-poetic type; a little weird but in a friendly way. Not like that crazy Sanskrit teacher we had.

You know what Sanskrit teachers are like. There are two kinds. One type, he smiles in a sad way as he writes declensions on the blackboard for the millionth time, his chalk squeaks—balak-*am*, balak-*au*, balak-*aha*—and the boys pass notes and make jokes while his back is turned, and they don't care if he minds.

The *other* type? Oh . . . you don't want to mess with this guy. This guy has the ancient fires of the Vedas in his eyes, he burns. No squeaks in his class, just terrified boys.

It was the second kind that came into our classroom that afternoon. It was the period after lunch, everyone was a little sweaty from football, they were still joking about Kiran or Arun or whatever his name was—one little kid, only four feet tall; he was tiny in every way; he had a very round head and he wore very round glasses. Someone had said, 'Hey, Lollipop!'

It was just the kind of stupid joke that everyone finds hilarious. Not me. 'Hey!' I said. 'Keep quiet, class has started!'

*

See, I didn't care about Kiran—or Arun—he was a mean guy. One time, when we were all the same size, he sat on Bodi.

Bodi was not the kind of guy you could sit on. That time, though, I guess we were eight, and he'd come to school with his head shaved. I don't know what it was, maybe some temple visit or someone died. When I saw him, I laughed. 'Look at you, *bodi*,' I said.

It was just a joke, but everyone latched on to it. Whole morning they called him Bodi, until even the teachers smiled. He kept touching the top of his head, but other than that, you couldn't tell he was getting upset. You never could, with Bodi.

Kiran—or Arun—got in on it late, at lunchtime. He was too excited. 'Bodi-bodi! Bodi-bodi!' He was *bouncing* with the fun of it. By now, Bodi was weak from pretending he didn't care. He turned to walk away, but Kiran-Arun pushed out his little leg and tripped him—I saw it with my own eyes—then he sat on him and patted Bodi's bald head.

Short term, this got him some laughs; long term, it was a big mistake. The next day, I don't know how, Bodi owned his nickname; he was strutting the corridors, wearing a hoodie over his uniform, walking like Salman Khan. But Kiran-Arun? Never grew another inch.

*

Anyway, Bodi ignored him after that, ignored him like a sheet of glass. Even now, in class, when everyone was making their stupid lollipop joke, Bodi was doing his own thing. Just talking and laughing with the boys sitting near him.

'Hey!' I said to the boys who were making the most noise. 'Shuttup, siddown!'

I was the class monitor, this was my job. Everyone knew this. If they became class monitor, they would have to do the same. So I really don't know why Bodi called out just then, 'DJ Darshan, down-down!'

That's me, Devjoti Darshan, DJ for short. Bodi had given me that nickname, it made me sound cool.

I don't know why he shouted like that. There were protests those days, on every other street. Protests

against the government, down-down! Protests against
the laws it made, hai-hai! Protests against the prime
minister, murdabad!

'DJ Darshan, down-down!'

'SHUT-tup!' I said. 'I'm going to write all your
names.'

That was my power, as monitor. I could write down
a boy's name, so the teacher who came in would know
who'd been making the most mischief.

I turned to the blackboard now, chalk in my
hand.

'DJ Darshan murdabad!'

It was a joke now, the class joined in. 'DJ Darshan,
hai-hai! DJ Darshan murdabad! DJ Darshan down-down!'

If it was some simple sort of mischief, you only
wrote the name. For anything more, you added a plus
sign. Shouting across the class—plus. Walking across
the class—plus-plus. Throwing balls, shooting paper
darts across the class—plus-plus-plus.

I wrote Bodi's name and I drew a long line after
it, all the way across the blackboard. Then I slashed it
with my chalk, plus+plus, plus+plus, *plusplusplusplus*. It
looked like a scar with stitches.

I was putting in the very last cut, at the very end of
the board, almost on its wooden frame—*DJ Darshan,
have some shame*!

There was a sudden hush.

The Sanskrit teacher walked up to me and took the chalk from my hand. He was a new one, this teacher, a skinny fellow with a long nose. When he took the chalk from me, I felt his skin, it was the skin of an old man, the skin of an onion. Dry, breaking.

'So many crosses,' he said. 'Who is this boy? Come in front!'

Bodi got up. Already, at thirteen, he was as tall as the teacher. He came up and looked at me for a second. He had a half-smile on his face, but he wasn't smiling at me; that was just how his face worked. He couldn't help it.

'What do you want?' said the teacher, and he put the duster on the desk before him. Then he reached into his pocket and took out a bunch of keys, held with a bottle-opener keychain. 'What do you want? Duster or keychain?'

I was standing right there. Bodi looked down at the teacher, then at the desk. I saw a very slight nod of his head. 'Keychain,' he said.

*

One time, when we were ten, Bodi came and stayed at my house for three days. I didn't want him to. 'Where will he sleep?' I said.

'In your room, don't be selfish,' my mother said.

'But Ma . . .!'

'Stop it. You know what the situation is.'

I knew what the situation was. Bodi's father didn't live with them. He came once or twice in a month, and stayed a day or two. Bodi's mother would talk to mine. Once I heard her say, 'Everyone told me I was making a mistake. I wish . . .'. Then she started crying, and Ma caught me staring and made a sharp sign with her head. *Go.*

Still. I didn't want Bodi in my bed. I knew he would break my toys; that is how Bodi was—*rough*. We fought all the time and my mother would shout at us, 'Stop it. Say sorry! Is this how you treat your friend?'

We said sorry. *Bam.* He would punch my arm, sorry. *Bam.* I would have him in a headlock, sorry. *Bam.* He would push me to the floor, sorry. *Bam.*

In bed, it was impossible. Kick, sorry, *bam*, pillow, push, sorry, *whack*, sorry, grunt, sorry, *hrrr!*

My mother would send my father in to shout, 'If I hear one more sound, I'll throw you both in the dustbin!' But we would keep tugging and pulling, grunting under our breath, until we were exhausted. It was only then that we slept.

One night, there was a *ptrr-ptrr* outside the window. '*Macha!*' said Bodi. He could say macha in a hundred different ways. Excited macha. Impatient macha. Pleading, wheedling, hey-y-y-y macha. Now he was wide awake, alert. '*Macha!*'

Ptrr.

'Ghost, goonda, thief!' said Bodi. 'Open the curtain. See.'

I didn't want to open my eyes. 'No,' I said.

'Come with me, macha. We'll see together.'

'No.'

'Open it!'

'No!'

He took my hand in his. 'Jo dara so mara,' he said. 'You want to be scared your whole life or what?'

We crept to the window and touched the curtain with our fingers, parting the cloth gingerly. We looked into a pair of round, yellow eyes. Big owl eyes.

I had never seen an owl before. Bodi's grip on my hand grew tight. 'Macha,' he said, 'we are going to die.'

'Shut up.'

'It's true,' he said. 'One time, this owl came to my house. Next day itself my grandfather died.'

'Don't tell lies,' I said. But I wasn't feeling so sure.

'Make it go away, macha. Please.'

The owl was staring right back at us, looking annoyed.

'Shoo!' I said. 'Shoo-shoo!'

It rose a little in the air and fell down again. Its talons scraped the windowsill, and a little rubble fell down. *Ptrrr.*

'It can't fly,' I said. 'It's broken. Let me . . .'. I touched the window to open it, and Bodi grabbed my hand.

'No!' he said, 'Don't let it in!'

I could see in his face, he was really afraid—I had never seen him be afraid like that, not even when CCTV Uncle set his dog on him.

*

CCTV Uncle had a house right next to the park where we played cricket and football and sometimes, when the girls made us, hide-and-seek. CCTV would watch us through his thick glasses, bent in his chair with a stinky old dog by his side, waiting and watching, watching and waiting, to *catch* us.

'Oh!' he would say on the phone to our parents, in his trembling voice, 'Siva was using such a filthy word today, I cannot repeat it, ma. Pasha was *pounding* on the flowers, I couldn't believe my eyes. Your little daughter, ma, shouting like a rowdy.'

One time, we crept under the hedge by his verandah. Bodi's mother had given him an old phone. That entire evening, he'd been showing it off. He took it out now and played the sound of crashing glass.

'Ayappa!' said CCTV Uncle. 'What have you done, you stupid woman?'

We played it again, as loud as we could.

'Ayyo! Breaking the whole kitchen or what? I'll take it from your salary, I'm warning you.'

We played it again. This time, CCTV Uncle's voice grew tentative. 'Sushma . . .?'

It seemed like we might bring the whole world crashing down, just us, four boys on a lawn with our hands on each other's mouths to keep the laughter from coming out. Bodi couldn't resist it for long.

'Sushmaaaa . . .' he said, imitating the old man's falsetto.

'Sush-*maaaa* . . .' The rest of us joined him.

'Rascals!' We could hear the creak of CCTV Uncle's chair, the tap-tap of his cane on the cement floor. 'Ruffians, villains, rowdies!'

Some days later, our ball went into his garden. He wouldn't give it back. 'What, Uncle? Give the ball, no, Uncle?'

'Get off or I'll send the dog after you,' he said.

'Send the dog with the ball, Uncle,' I said.

Maybe I was inspired by Bodi, maybe I was jealous of him. His trick with the breaking glass had made him a star. All the kids said to each other: 'That Bodi! Heard what he did?'

'Send the dog with the ball, Uncle. He can be wicketkeeper, Uncle!'

Everyone laughed. Bodi put one hand on my shoulder, the other on his hip, leaning on me like a hero. 'Hey, Uncle, give us the ball, no?' he said.

'You want your ball, is it?' CCTV Uncle got up from his chair. 'Your father is President of America, that you'll throw your ball where you like, troubling the whole colony?'

I felt Bodi's fingers tense. 'Why, Uncle, your father was an owl or what, watching everything with big-big eyes?'

CCTV Uncle rushed out of his gate. I took a step back, without thinking. *Just a joke, Uncle,* I could have said. I took a step back and Bodi's hand fell from my shoulder—we were all a step behind him when the old man stumbled out and slapped his face. That old dog of his got up, too, and ran out, barking.

This time, though, CCTV had messed up. Bodi's mother called him before he could call her. 'Whatever it is, sir,' she said, 'whatever the child may have done, I do not think he deserves to get rabies.'

She wouldn't listen to his justifications or complaints. 'What sort of man sends a dog to bite a child? I should call the police!'

*

Now, as the owl fluttered its wings once again, I could tell Bodi was wishing for his mother.

'Jo dara so mara,' I said, and I said it with a little gloat, I admit. 'It's just a stupid bird.'

I pulled my right hand out of his; he wouldn't let go of my left. I pushed the window open slightly, and then I could see more clearly: it wasn't that its wing was broken, it was only caught in some little wire. All I had to do was nudge it . . .

Bodi's fingers tightened around my hand.

'All I have to do . . .' I stuck my hand out of the window, fingers wide. The owl fluttered again, I tugged at the pipe. 'There!'

I looked at Bodi, 'See? It's gone.'

He held my hand all the way back to bed, and he was holding it, still, in the morning.

*

That was what . . . four years ago? *Again*, I thought, *he's doing it again.* Why did he choose the bottle-opener? *Jo dara so mara, macha.* What a stupid choice, I could feel it, the keys; my belly grew tight, I thought I would pee. No, no, sir, it was just a joke, I should have said, just a joke—in a second the teacher had trapped two of Bodi's fingers in the keychain. And wrenched.

'Aaaie!'

My eyes fell to the floor; I didn't dare look up.

'Go,' said the teacher.

From where I sat, I could see Bodi's face. I had never seen him cry.

As soon as the class ended, I rushed to him. Half the class had crowded around his desk. His hand was swollen, like an orange.

'He broke your fingers, man,' said somebody. We had three more classes to go. 'He broke your fingers, man.'

'Hey, Bodi,' I said, 'I'll take you to the nurse, macha, come.'

He didn't look at me. He didn't move.

The next day, Bodi came to school with his hand in plaster, and his mother by his side. She marched into the principal's office, not bothering to ask if he was free.

When Bodi came back to class, he had his strut again. 'You should have seen that fellow's face!' There was a crowd of boys around him, lapping at his words. 'Arre, you should have seen his face when Amma started. *It is a disgrace!* Fellow was falling at my feet!'

I put a hand on his shoulder, everyone was patting him like he'd scored a winning goal. He looked at me sideways and shrugged my hand away.

I didn't know how to say sorry. In the lunch break, I went up to him and punched his arm, just a little, very gently. 'Sorry,' I said and waited for it. *Bam.*

He didn't even look at me.

*

I wished I could go back in time and *fix* it. Just a week before that Sanskrit class, Bodi and I were riding our cycles in Cubbon Park, yelling *chakka-chakka-chakka* at all the transgenders, giggling when they glared at us, raised their hands as if to beat us; speeding away when they shouted, 'Go back to your mothers, you silly boys!'

Back home, Bodi said, 'You would be pretty as a girl, macha.'

'What're you talking?'

'No, believe me. Look.'

He went into his mother's room and brought out her lipstick and kajal.

'It's not funny, man.'

'I'll do it, wait, you'll see.'

He put the lipstick on himself, and lined his eyes. He knew exactly how to do it; his face changed immediately. He looked older, like he knew all the secrets, like he could grant wishes.

'What do you say, macha?'

Even his voice had changed. There was a rasp to it, a glitch, like when something goes wrong with the sound in a film. 'What do you say?'

I couldn't say anything, I nodded my head. He took me by the chin and dabbed the colour on my lips, the black on my eyes. 'Come on,' he said, 'let's compare who's best.'

We went to the mirror and it broke the spell. We were only two boys, after all, with very red lips and very dark eyes. We laughed. 'Jackass,' I said.

Bodi ran to his mother's room and brought out two saris. 'Come on, come on!'

We wrapped the saris around ourselves, round and round and tuck and throw, and we sashayed up and down the corridors like the transgenders on the streets.

We were laughing, we were calling out insults, we were flirting with the saucepan in the kitchen, with the backs of the dining chairs. Bodi put on music and we danced, shaking our hips like in music videos.

That's when I tripped. My sari was unravelling, it caught in my feet and I fell headlong into Bodi's arms.

That's when he kissed me.

I didn't know what to do, so I left. Later that night, Bodi sent me a message, that dancing girl emoji in the red dress. I didn't know what to do, so I didn't reply.

*

DJ Darshan, down-down!

All week after, Bodi was weird, saying things in weird ways. Like when I scored a goal, he said, 'Pelé-style!', but it didn't sound like he was being nice. It sounded mean. And when he started that chant . . . I was so angry by then, I could have punched him in the face. *DJ Darshan, have some shame!* But all I did was make some marks on a board.

After that Sanskrit class, Bodi stopped talking to me. I became like Lollipop, a sheet of glass.

It went on for weeks. At first, I pretended I didn't care. It wasn't my fault. It was Bodi who made me angry. It was Bodi who chose the keychain. It was Bodi who brought out the lipstick. *He* was the one who messed things up, *I* was the one who saved him from the owl.

But I couldn't pretend for very long. There was never a time that Bodi and I weren't friends. I didn't know what it could be, to be without him. Everything about me felt dull, except the pain in my gut. I had not meant for his fingers to break. I had not meant to fall in his arms. If only I could tell him: it wasn't my fault. If only I could tell him, I felt like a loudspeaker without its song.

But how does a sheet of glass explain such things? It was impossible.

A month, two months—eventually I stopped looking at him and hoping he would look back. I started eating my lunch in the classroom, alone, putting my head on the desk and closing my eyes, pretending I was tired or unwell, that's why I couldn't play. Not that anyone cared—the whole class held Bodi's broken fingers against me.

On the last day of class that year, I was sitting like this, when Bodi walked in and ruffled my hair.

'Sleeping all day, macha,' he said.

That was it. We never dressed up in his mother's saris again, he never kissed me again and we never became friends in the old way again. Still, it was better than nothing; even if, sometimes, it felt like he let me back in out of pity.

*

It has been years since we left school. We follow each other on things. He wears a sari in his DPs, and a half-smile. Some days, I imagine sending him a message.

Maybe I would write, *Not all teachers are so bad. Remember that history fellow we had, with all the questions?*

The weirdest was the time he said—out of nowhere—'Can anyone tell me: what is a mistake?'

Everyone tried, of course. 'Telling lies, sir!', 'Mistaken identity, sir!', 'God is watching, sir!'

'Listen,' he'd said, 'there are two kinds of mistakes. One is technical, the other is moral. Do you understand? If I say two plus two equals five, what will you say?'

'Wrong, sir, wrong!'

'You could say wrong. You could say that I've made an error in my calculation. Do you understand? A technical mistake, you slap your forehead. *Oh!* You erase it, you *fix* it. But what about mistakes that cannot be calculated; mistakes that can only be judged? What about mistakes that cannot be fixed or erased; mistakes that can only be forgiven or punished? A machine will tell you the right answer to two and two, but who will you trust to tell you the right thing to do? Who will you allow to judge you? How much will you dare judge the world around you? And how willing will you be to judge your own selves?'

We had laughed, indulging him, turning to look at each other smiling.

Now I imagine sending Bodi a message. *Is there a third kind of mistake? The kind that friends make?*

I imagine his reply.

I wrote this story as part of a theatre workshop conducted by Sylvie Baillon at the Katkatha Studio, New Delhi. I am grateful to Samta Shikhar, who invited me to the workshop to develop her idea of a play around the theme of 'mistakes'. This story grew out of the resulting two weeks of conversations and improvisations with Samta Shikhar, Shrunga B.V., and Subhashim Goswami.

The Rumour about Mona

Neha Singh

Mona pretended to study in her room but waited desperately for her phone to ring. Her phone was far away, in the living room. Her mother had a rule, you see: No phones in the room during study hours. Not that it helped much right now. Instead of focusing on organic chemistry, all Mona could think about was that phone call she was waiting for.

The phone rang and Mona raced to see if it was him.

It wasn't.

She picked up the phone in exasperation.

'Hey, how did you get the answer for the integration question number 4, step by step?' Paro asked.

Oh no, this could take forever.

'Oh that?'

Not now, Paro.

'Can I WhatsApp you? Later?'

'No, no, just tell me on the phone, na. I'm here with my laptop.' Paro could be persistent.

'Oh, question number 4? Total bouncer. I didn't get it either.' Mona hated lying to her friends, but in matters of Utmost Importance, it had to be done.

'Shut up! How have you reached problem 17 when you couldn't get 4?' Paro was getting on her nerves now.

Mona could hear the 'call waiting' beep in the background, which was almost as loud as her pounding heart.

Unknown number. She hadn't saved it in case her parents checked. She didn't need to anyway. She had memorized it the day he had given it to her.

'I gotta go!' she said, cutting the call before Paro could protest any further.

She took a deep breath and said, 'Hello?' She winced—it had come off a little more frantic than she had hoped.

'Hi . . . Mona?' a dreamy voice asked. It was him.

'This is she.' Mona prayed he couldn't hear the blaring thumps of her heartbeat.

'Hey, this is Zafar. What's up? How was your day?' he asked.

'We had a double period of physics. So, you can imagine.' Mona tried being casual.

'Hahaha. I love physics!' Zafar said.

'Well, everyone is not a genius like you.'

'Hardly a genius. I just manage my time well.'

Oof, why did he have to be so gorgeous and so modest?

'So, why does the head boy of the school want to take me out on a date?' Mona dared to be brave.

'Because you are cute and talented, and I would like to get to know you better. And that's not possible at school. And we have chatted enough on Insta, haven't we?'

Gorgeous, modest AND honest, sigh!

'But you know, I always thought you were dating Misha, from 12 B.'

'Misha? How did you reach that conclusion?' He was chuckling.

'She's in all your Insta stories.' Mona winced again. She had just revealed, unwittingly, that she stalked him on social media.

'Incorrect. Misha *tags* me in all her stories!' Zafar seemed to find her jealous tone rather sweet. Mona was secretly delighted.

'Same thing. So, nothing is going on between you two?'

'No way. We are buddies.'

'Fine, so what were you saying?'

She saw her mom popping her head out from behind her laptop to suss out who she was talking to.

'Who is it? Why are you whispering?' Mom raised her eyebrow.

'I am not! I am just talking to Paro.' Mona covered the phone's microphone with one hand and lied through her teeth.

'Okay. Finish the call quickly and go help Dad in the kitchen. You know how messy he can get.'

Mom was typing again, but she had turned off the music. Mothers are always up to all sorts of tricks!

'Okay, so what do you wanna do tomorrow?' Mona whispered into the phone.

'I was thinking, let's catch a movie at Sangam?' Zafar suggested. Sangam was the only decent movie theatre in Mathura.

'No way! That's boring. Let's do something more fun, more adventurous.' Mona said, talking quickly.

'I thought you liked movies.'

He doesn't have a plan B?

'I like movies! But this is going to be my first date ever. And I want it to be special. I don't want to grow old and tell my grandkids that the first date I ever went on was to watch a movie at Sangam.' There, she had said it.

'Hahaha. You are funny.'

'I am, and cute too, remember? So, now, think fast.' Mona was whispering furiously now.

'You suggest something . . .'

'Um, Dad bought a new fishing rod from Denmark. Let's go to the Yamuna and try to catch fish?'

'Are you serious?'

'Never been more serious in my life.'

'Okay, okay. See you at 3 p.m.?'

'Yeah, and park your scooter near Sanjeev's house. I am telling my folks that I am going over to Paro's for combined studies.'

Mona had figured out the logistics way in advance, in the eternal hope of this very day.

*

'Study hard! Be back before seven . . .' Dad called after Mona as she stepped out, 'and keep your phone charged.'

The large silver hoops in Mona's ears shimmered in the winter afternoon. Her hair was still a little wet and fell around her face in loose curls. She had quietly taken the fishing rod from the storeroom, wrapped it in a plastic bag and stuffed it into her tennis bag.

Her dark, big eyes lit up as soon as she saw Zafar's sky-blue scooter whizz by. Zafar looked every bit as dreamy as Mona had imagined he would on this magnificent day.

'Shall we?' Zafar smiled that irresistible smile as he handed her an extra helmet. She had longed to sit on this antique scooter and hold Zafar as tightly as she could even before they'd started chatting on Instagram. She was the luckiest girl ever.

'What did you say about the tennis bag?' Zafar inquired.

'I told Mom that Paro and I might play for a bit, just to refresh ourselves. Now let's go!' Mona said, butterflies fluttering in her tummy.

*

The desi fish in the Yamuna clearly weren't attracted to the Denmark-made fishing rod. But who cared about catching fish? Mona hummed a tune as she made videos of the river. Thankfully, her family wasn't on Instagram. They wouldn't know she was not really doing combined studies with Paro.

Zafar and Mona couldn't have been happier to just be in each other's company. She wished she could take a selfie with Zafar and put it on her Insta feed, but she didn't dare.

Not yet, at least.

Hearing her hum, Zafar said, 'You should participate in the solo singing competition.'

'You think so?' Mona was secretly thrilled.

'You have such a sweet voice.'

So generous with compliments!

'Thank you. And that dance you all did on 'Jai Ho' for 15 August. Did you choreograph it?' Mona didn't want this day to end.

'Yeah, you saw it?' Zafar asked.

'Of course. You were amazing.'

Something tugged at the fishing rod suddenly.

Mona shrieked in excitement and said, 'Help me pull this thing up!' All her other fishing adventures had been with Dad, who had always helped her wind up the fishing rod.

Zafar got up and stood behind her. The fish was heavy and tugging furiously at the rod. Zafar kept his hand on top of hers and rotated the handle anticlockwise. Mona could feel the warmth of Zafar's body against hers. His face was so close to the nape of her neck that his hot breath bristled the hairs on her skin.

She wanted a remote control to simply pause this moment forever. But there was a fish that needed to be pulled out of the water.

Except, it wasn't a fish.

Zafar burst into peals of laughter as Mona pulled out an old tyre that probably belonged to a jeep or a tractor. She turned around to look at him and then, letting go of the rod, looked him in the eye. And just like that, they were in an embrace. They held each other, first gently and then a little tighter. Time stopped as Mona and Zafar melted into each other's bodies against the setting sun, their soft skins turning a pink-orange blush.

They stood on that little rock, in a tight hug for what seemed like eternity, while the Yamuna gently gurgled beside them and the tyre still tugged at the fishing rod.

Her phone rang.

Mom.

Mona cut the call and started texting her mother rapidly.

Just finishing physics. Took longer than expected.
Be home in half an hour.

'It's dark,' she looked up from her phone and said reluctantly.

'Time to head back.' Zafar said, almost in a whisper.

'Ice cream at Baskin Robbins before that?' She needed just about any reason to delay the end. *And any decent date should ideally end at the brand new and only Baskin Robbins in town. They had thirty-one flavours!*

Her phone pinged. *Mom!*

You were supposed to be home at 7! It's 7.10!?!

'Sure!' Zafar said, walking back to his scooter.

Mona put her phone on silent, picked up the fishing rod and got on the scooter. She held on to Zafar as they headed back. No one in the world could ruin this day.

Her grip around Zafar was just a little bit tighter than before, even though he rode as slow as he possibly could. Mona's mind was fuzzy and Zafar's body so close to hers was making it fuzzier.

The scooter spluttered precariously for a minute before it came to a complete halt.

The loyal companion and stoic guard to Zafar and Mona's romance had turned rogue.

Oh no!

'I know! The school gate is almost here. Let's just drag it till school. You park your scooter there. Then we can walk to Baskin Robbins and walk back home,' Mona suggested.

Thank God for small towns where everything is just about walking distance.

*

'Chocolate?' Zafar asked as they found themselves staring at an endless list of ice cream flavours.

'No, choco chip,' Mona replied.

So much for thirty-one flavours.

'So, you think you have a good story for your grandkids now?' Zafar teased Mona as they walked out with their ice creams.

'Better than ever. Especially when you include the tyre!' Mona laughed as she licked the melted ice cream off her hand.

While making their way back towards the school gate, Zafar was still licking off some of the ice cream from his fingers.

'May I?' Mona asked gingerly. 'Since I wasn't offered even one bite.'

Zafar looked deeply into her kajal-lined eyes and extended his hand. Mona held his hand and licked the ice cream off his fingers. Zafar felt a sweat break out, even though it was the dead of winter.

Suddenly, a phone torch flashed in their faces.

'Aye, who is that? Zafar? And who is this girl?' a voice pierced through what Mona thought was going to be the perfect end to their dreamlike first date.

'This is Mona. 10 C. Why, sir?'

Mr A.P. Singh, their chemistry teacher, stood in front of them now, wearing a monkey cap and a suspicious look.

'Zafar, I did not expect you to stoop so low. *Chhii chhii chhiii.* Parking your scooter here and then going off into the bushes . . .' he barked into the night.

How dare he reduce the wondrous evening into something utterly disgusting?

Mona was quick to react.

'Excuse me, sir. Please don't use such language. We were just at Baskin Robbins. Getting ice cream.' Mona's voice shook a bit, but she stood her ground.

'Why park your scooter here then? I have punctured both tyres, by the way. Wanted to make sure you couldn't just run away after your dirty deed.' A.P. Singh spoke as if he had done something commendable.

Zafar finally found his voice.

'Sir, with all due respect, the scooter stopped working, so instead of dragging it all the way we thought we can leave it here, and just walk to the ice cream shop.'

'We thought it would be safe here. But clearly, we were mistaken,' Mona added.

'Tell these stories to your parents when I call them. You, tell me your father's number.' A.P. Singh pointed at Mona, hell-bent on ripping their date and their hearts apart.

Mona froze.

She couldn't let her mom and dad know she was out with Zafar. She was supposed to be with Paro, studying physics.

Zafar took his phone out of his pocket. 'Sir, I am calling my dad. This is just ridiculous.' He knew the situation needed to be handled intelligently.

'Please, my parents shouldn't know,' Mona whispered as she clasped Zafar's hand.

'No whispering! And no holding hands! Shameless girl,' A.P. Singh shouted.

'Don't worry,' Zafar said and held her hand exactly the way her dad would when she was scared after a nightmare.

After what seemed like a lifetime, Zafar's dad appeared in his car.

Mona had braced herself for the worst.

Please don't slap Zafar. Please don't slap Zafar. Please be . . . Zafar's dad interjected just then. 'Get in, kids. You should have called me earlier. I would have dropped the car off for the two of you.' Zafar's dad seemed to react as if nothing had happened.

A.P. Singh was as shocked as Mona.

'Sir, your son was up to no good. He was behind the bushes with this class 10 girl and . . .' A.P. Singh clearly wasn't satisfied with the misery he had already caused.

Zafar's father stopped him mid-sentence, 'I will ask my son for the details of what happened today, sir. Why don't you go home now? It's freezing outside. And I will send someone to get the scooter. Goodnight.'

Mona got into the car quickly and pulled the windows up. Suddenly the night felt extremely cold. How was she going to stop Zafar's dad from informing her parents? Her parents wouldn't take as kindly to her, especially since she had lied to them. If they got to know she had been to the river and was hanging out with a boy, they might cancel all her outings from now on.

A.P. Singh tapped on the window.

Mona pulled it down nervously.

'I am not letting this go so easily. The school has a certain code of ethics and I will make sure I inform the principal. Let him decide after that,' A.P. Singh spoke with a calm surety.

'Do what you want, sir. I did no wrong.' Mona was livid, but she looked at her sweaty palms and thought about what would happen when the principal, the entire school and eventually her parents heard about her date with Zafar.

She pulled out her phone. Seven missed calls from Mom. It was 8 p.m.

Oh, damn you, first date.

It had suddenly become way more (mis)adventurous than Mona had anticipated, or desired.

'Should I come in and explain things to your parents?' Zafar's dad was trying to calm the two down.

'No, Uncle. That won't be necessary. Thank you,' Mona blurted.

'Don't worry, Mona, we didn't do anything wrong. There's nothing to be stressed about.' Zafar looked over at the back seat, where Mona sat clinging to the door, and reached for her hand.

*

Mona entered the house, terrified.

Mom was silent while Dad was in the kitchen.

The calm before the storm.

'Sorry I got late. Paro's mom was making gajar ka halwa for us.' She seated herself at the dinner table and began drinking her palak soup in quiet contemplation.

Mona wished she could tell her parents what had happened. How would she explain the web of lies she had created? Not in her wildest dreams would her parents have allowed her to go on a date!

'Why weren't you taking Mom's calls? Paro also didn't pick up—we were worried!' Dad said.

'We were studying and the phones were a distraction. We kept them on silent so we could finish homework as soon as possible.'

Yet another lie. Good going, Mona.

'What's the point of giving you a phone when you don't bother to pick up our calls?' Mom spoke, after an agonizing wait.

'I texted you. Why do you have to call me a million times? I am fifteen, not five!'

'What's going on? I hope you aren't becoming like those backbencher types who just take pouty selfies and roam around with useless boys. You have to get above 90 per cent this year too. It's a board year.' Dad said this in a tone he rarely used.

'What's getting 90 per cent got to do with having boyfriends?' Mona's armpits were sweaty now.

'This is no age for such things. Girls who get involved in all that nonsense end up being nothing but entertainment for gossipmongers. Get into a good college in Delhi and then do what you want.' Mom was looking pointedly at Mona.

Do they know what had happened? Were they psyching her out to tell them the truth? Mona only wanted to hug her mother and tell her what that awful A.P. Singh had said about her. But she knew there would be repercussions. Severe repercussions.

'Hmmm,' Mona answered without looking up.

'If this continues, I will take your phone away.' Dad gave her an ultimatum, before continuing to slurp on his soup.

It had all been going so perfectly. Even the minor hiccups of the tyre instead of the fish and the scooter conking off hadn't made a dent in their happiness. And that moment when they'd hugged on that little rock! Mona knew Zafar felt the same as she did. She could tell. The way he had looked at her with a deep longing and the affection with which he had held her hand. It was so evident that what they felt for each other was love.

If only she had reached home on time. If only she had not asked Zafar to park the scooter at the school gate. If only they had never decided to go to Baskin Robbins. But she wanted to be with Zafar for just a little while longer. What was so sinful about that?

Wrapped in her razai, Mona whispered into her almost-confiscated phone, 'Hello.'

'Hi. Is everything okay at home?' Zafar whispered back.

'Not really, but I managed. I am scared about school tomorrow.'

'Me too. I am so sorry, Mona.'

'Why are you sorry? It's all that idiot A.P.'s fault. And now he is going to rat us out to Princi.' Mona was gritting her teeth.

'Don't worry. We'll figure something out. This shouldn't be happening to you.'

'It's not just happening to me. It's happening to both of us, Zafar!' said Mona, a little confused.

'Of course! But you know how things are. When something like this happens, people just want to point fingers at the girl.' Zafar sounded apologetic.

'That's nonsense. It's not like I dragged you out to come with me. Both of us made a choice, so we are in this together, fifty-fifty.'

'I know. But that's not how things usually work. Like, I could tell my parents I was going out with a girl, but you couldn't. For girls it's much tougher to tell their parents, at least that's true in a lot of cases. Anyway, don't worry. I will handle this at school tomorrow,' said Zafar.

Her stomach suddenly felt queasy and she wanted to throw up.

'You all right?'

'I am not feeling too well. Maybe I will just bunk school tomorrow,' Mona stuttered.

'No, you won't. You will come to school and we will handle it. I won't let anything happen to you, okay?'

'I don't know, Zafar. It was all so surreal and then everything just got destroyed.'

'Well, now you have so much more to tell your grandkids!'

'Shut up. All this just makes me feel so dirty.'

Mona was fumbling to express what she felt.

'It's not you who is dirty. It's that dumbass A.P. Singh whose head is full of shit. You are the most intelligent, engaging and fun person I have hung out with.'

Sigh. Keep talking.

'Let's just be done with whatever happens tomorrow. Then we'll have enough time to plan our second-best date,' Zafar laughed.

They hung up, but Mona felt a bit unsettled with what Zafar had said.

Why could Zafar tell his parents, but she couldn't tell hers? Would A.P. Singh make her the sole target of the entire episode? Will it all become about how 'bad' Mona is? Will they shame her? What if the principal asks her to come on stage in the morning assembly and confess to the whole school what had transpired between her and Zafar the day before?

*

Mona remembered everything from the previous night in an agonizing flash when she woke up. Her stomach twisted into multiple knots and her heart jumped to her throat.

'Wish I could skip this day and wake up tomorrow,' she wrote on her Insta story.

Paro messaged her almost immediately.

'All okay, sweety? Your mom was calling me like crazy yesterday.'

'Will tell you at school. Big drama.'

Mona called out to her mother. 'Mom, is it okay if I don't go to school today?'

Mom popped in with a warm glass of milk, looking worried.

'What happened?' she asked.

'Nothing. Stomach is hurting and I feel nauseous. I will be fine if I can rest it out today.'

Mona turned to her side, so that Mom wouldn't see her face.

'Period cramps?' Mom asked.

'No.'

If only Mom knew that sometimes a heartache could be more devastating than anything else, even period cramps.

'Paro and you ate that awful dahi chaat again, didn't you?' Mom checked Mona's forehead for fever.

The heat that's awaiting in school couldn't compare to any fever.

'Yeah, we did. Sorry,' Mona said. As Dad walked in with two cups of tea, Mona asked him, 'Will you make me some moong-dal khichdi for lunch?'

'If you keep missing school like this, how will you clear IIT?'

'They don't teach IIT courses in school, Dad!' Mona watched her tone, even though she was irritated.

'Let her be. But make sure you get all your notes and homework for the day from Paro.' Mom was unusually kind today.

Thank God for small mercies.

Mom took Mona's phone and walked out the door.

'Mom, my phone!' Mona yelled.

'Thank your lucky stars I let you lock it,' Mom spoke with a deadpan look.

'Yes, yes, okay, now let me sleep some more.' Mona ducked her head under her blanket.

Enveloped in the darkness of the razai, she felt safe. But what about Zafar? What will he think of her when she doesn't show up at school? That she was a coward, a flake, someone he couldn't trust? And what about that moron A.P. Singh? He would think that he had won and she had lost when she had done no wrong.

What had she done that was so wrong? Mona suddenly felt singed with fury. She wasn't a coward. She was brave and right and she didn't need to be scared. And she needed to be there with Zafar to tell the truth. And defend herself. She wasn't going to let that nincompoop get away with this nonsense.

'Mom! Dad! Getting ready in a minute,' Mona shouted as she jumped out of bed and rushed to the loo.

'Hurry or you will miss the bus,' Dad yelled back.

'Don't worry. I will cycle to school if I miss the bus. But no way am I missing school today!' Mona replied as she swung her school bag on her back, stuffed her phone into her pocket and rushed out.

'I have a feeling she is hiding something from us. I hope it's not some boyfriend nonsense,' Mom said to Dad as she watched Mona run towards the front gate.

'Chhi. She is too young for all that. You are just paranoid. She has only the IIT entrance exam on her mind!' Dad said, pleased.

*

Mona stood in the school ground, eyes closed, hands folded in prayer, invoking Ma Durga for strength. The others sang the school prayer with as much enthusiasm as they could muster on a cold, foggy, dreary Monday morning.

Her eyes were searching for Zafar. They were alone, together in their love-crime and ready to face the sentence, hands clasped in solidarity.

She couldn't see him anywhere. Not on the podium where he usually stood during assemblies, not checking the students for proper uniforms or polished shoes. He wasn't even in the 12 B queue. Where was he? Maybe he couldn't sleep well either and was just rushing to school on his scooter—their sky-blue co-conspirator in this entire episode.

Mona's pulse quickened when she saw the principal come on stage. What was he going to say? And where the hell was Zafar? She wasn't ready to go up on stage alone. He said they would handle everything together and now he wasn't here. She kept glancing at the school gate, hoping to catch a glimpse of his scooter.

A.P. Singh stared at her with raised eyebrows from across the school grounds. She wanted the earth to split open and swallow her. A.P. Singh took out his phone and started typing.

What is he up to? Is he broadcasting a message about us?

She looked around. She spotted a boy from class 11 looking at her. Did he know? She looked at her class teacher Mrs Bisht, who looked at her phone and then at Mona. Oh no. She really liked Mrs Bisht and didn't want to disappoint her. She glanced at the queue of 10 A. They were all staring at her.

Everyone knows!

There was a rumour going around about her. She was sure of it. A rumour about Mona. This couldn't be happening. The whole school knew A.P.'s version of the story. That Zafar and she had parked the scooter and had gone behind the bushes. Oh man, where was Zafar? She couldn't take it any more.

A scooter screeched to a halt at the main gate. She turned around to see Zafar walking towards her. She broke the queue and ran to him.

'ZAFARRRRRR!' she screamed.

The principal rushed off the stage. A.P. Singh tried blocking her way, but she pushed him aside and broke into a run. The guards tried making a human wall between her and Zafar, but she tore through that and ran into the outstretched arms of her hero, her love, her saviour. The whole school surrounded them.

'Save me,' she said and fell into Zafar's safe and strong arms.

'Hey, Mona, Mona . . .' Paro was nudging her arm.

It was a daydream. Or a daymare. Mona decided that she had to stop watching too many Hindi films. This wasn't a film and there was no Zafar here to save her. She peeked at A.P. Singh, who was still staring at her with eyebrows raised, from the corner of her eye.

Mona held her breath as she looked at Principal Bedi. His speech was over! With no mention of her.

Wait, what?

The students started dispersing to their classrooms. Paro tugged at her and whispered, 'Tell me about the drama, no? There is some rumour about you and Zafar. Apparently, A.P. Singh's son has been sending a photo around on WhatsApp. Look, I got it too!'

Mona took her phone. It was a blurry photo of Zafar and Mona on the scooter.

Principal Bedi walked past Mona and spoke quietly. 'See me in my office in five minutes.'

The nightmare was clearly still on. And still no sign of Zafar. Looked like it was time to be her own hero and save herself.

'Gotta go,' she said to a concerned Paro.

Mona walked with leaden legs what seemed like the shortest distance, and the longest distance ever, to Principal Bedi's office. She hadn't felt this vulnerable and alone ever. But she stood straight, her spine upright.

That dog A.P. Singh was there, smug with his little secret.

'Puttar, what happened yesterday?' Principal Bedi asked.

'Wait, sir. I have called her parents too. They must be on their way now,' A.P. Singh said with the most vicious smile ever.

Hot, salty tears blinded Mona for a moment and then she blinked them away. How will she face her parents? She felt faint.

Mom and Dad arrived, looking pale and confused. They gazed at everyone in the room and after what seemed like an eternity, Mom spoke.

'What has happened? Is Mona all right?'

Is this how the world ends?

'Oh, she is quite alright. Let's hear it from the horse's mouth, the events of yesterday, shall we?' A.P.'s words seemed grating in Mona's ears.

Mona's cheeks reddened and her heart threatened to pop out of her chest.

She said, 'Mom, Dad, I am really sorry for lying to you. I wasn't with Paro yesterday; I was with Zafar.'

Mom inhaled sharply and glared at her.

'Zafar and I went to the river and then to the ice cream shop. His scooter had broken down, so we left it at the school gate. When we returned from the shop to collect the scooter, Mr A.P. Singh flashed his torchlight at us and started shouting. He punctured the tyres on Zafar's scooter too. His son even took a picture of us and sent it to people,' Mona spoke softly.

'Sir, I know these boys and girls. They just want to do dirty things and they make up all these lies later.' A.P. the ape was relentless.

'First of all, with all due respect, please stop using the word 'dirty'. Second, Zafar and I are friends and what we do on a Sunday afternoon shouldn't be your concern, sir. Yes, I lied to my parents, but that's because I knew that if I'd told them the truth, they would never have let me go. I chose to spend the day with Zafar, and he with me.'

'But, puttar, it's not safe to be roaming around in the dark.' Principal Bedi looked genuinely concerned.

'Sir, the only time we felt unsafe yesterday was in the presence of Mr A.P. Singh.' Mona didn't know how she had found the strength to speak up and defend herself.

'Why did you have to lie to us? What have we ever done to make you feel like you can't tell us the truth?' Her father asked her with disappointment more than with anger.

This time it felt like Mona had been waiting to be asked this question her entire life. She felt something break within her.

'Dad, I am fifteen. Why can't I have even a little bit of privacy in my own home? I am constantly monitored. Both of you are always snooping around, eavesdropping and checking who I am talking to. On the one hand, you want me to get 90 per cent and crack IIT. You want me to be a grown-up about it and take charge of my future. I study very hard to do exactly that. But on the other hand, you treat me like I don't know right from wrong. You constantly breathe down my neck.'

'Look at how this girl is talking!' A.P. appeared shocked. But Mona couldn't care less now. She had to speak. It was now or never.

'Isn't it ironic that you consider me old enough to make the biggest decisions of my life, but not old enough to spend an evening with a friend who is a boy?' Mona's bright eyes lit up when she heard her own voice echo across the room.

'But, sir . . .' A.P. the ape began.

Mona wasn't finished yet.

'I want to ask you all. When we study together, play together and are friends at school, why is it wrong if we are attracted to each other or even just wish to hang out as friends? Why is it made out to be so criminal and shameful? And why hasn't Zafar been dragged in here too? Why just me and my parents? Sorry if I am out of line, but it's people like A.P. Singh sir who make it seem ugly and dirty, not us.'

Mona glanced at her parents and saw a difference in the way they looked at her now, like her words had made some sense to them. Like they wanted to smack A.P. across his face for what he had put her through. Will they speak up and defend her?

'I can't believe this girl is defending such behaviour . . . This is unacceptable in our society. And that too, with a Muslim boy . . . Sir . . . you know I don't believe in such things, but still, good Indian values need to be upheld under . . .'

Mona's mom cut in. 'Our daughter may have lied to us and I will have a talk with her separately. But as of now, I am truly disgusted with what Mr A.P. Singh has put my child through. Schools are supposed to provide a healthy environment for discourse. You don't know how these kinds of incidents can affect their vulnerable minds. What if she had taken a drastic step?'

Mona couldn't hold back her tears when she felt her dad's arms around her shoulder.

'You must apologize to her. And if I catch you harassing students again with your vile behaviour, I will . . . I will . . . you'll be sorry.' Mona had never seen her dad so livid.

'A.P. It's because of people like you that youngsters are scared of telling us the truth. They feel they can't share some things with us. We are supposed to be a child's allies and guides, not their abusers and harassers. I won't allow such regressive behaviour in my school. Take this as a warning.' Principal Bedi was savage.

A.P. didn't know what hit him. He was supposed to get brownie points for being a guardian of 'good Indian values' and now he was the guilty one?

'I . . . I . . . am sorry. But . . .' he started.

'Apologies aren't suffixed with "buts", A.P.' Principal Bedi interrupted.

'I . . . I am sorry, Mona,' he finally muttered.

'Mona, I want to clarify just one more thing. It's not like I wanted to call only you to the office and not Zafar. Zafar hasn't come to school today. If he had come, he would be here too. I wanted to hear all sides of the story. For me, all you kids are equal and equally important. Remember that, always.' The principal reassured her.

'And when Zafar comes in, remember to apologize to him too. Sorry, puttar, for putting you through this,' Principal Bedi touched the top of Mona's head gently as he spoke.

'Thank you, sir,' replied Mona.

'For?'

'For being the best principal ever.'

'Thank you for being a brave girl. Thank you for trusting me. And next time you want to go to the Yamuna to catch fish, tell me. I will tell you the best spot.'

Why didn't every school have a principal like Bedi sir?

Mona was too overwhelmed to speak as she stepped out of the principal's room. Her dad caught her hand.

'Can we just sit in the canteen for a bit?' Mom suggested.

The school canteen was empty except for the new temporary teacher typing away on her laptop.

'I can't believe you didn't tell us about such a big incident. We are always here for you, Mona,' Dad said.

'I know I should have . . . I just didn't know how you would . . .'

'I am still very upset with you. Why'd you think that we wouldn't protect you?' Mom was emotional. 'But I am also very proud of you, Mona. You said some very important things back there. We need to talk. We need to have an honest discussion. In the evening.'

Mona looked at her mom and said, 'I don't say this often, but I love you. And I love you too, Dad. Thank you for standing up for me.'

'Okay, now let her go back to class,' Mom said, wiping a tear.

'But this isn't over yet. Now run off to class and remember . . . IIT!' Dad kissed her on the forehead.

Mona walked slowly towards her class.

Weirdly, she felt much lighter. Like a load she had been carrying had been taken off her chest. She knew this was the beginning of a brand-new relationship with her parents and with her own self. She had initiated the process of demolishing that mountain of mistrust and fear that stood between her and them. Now she needed to flatten it, one step at a time. She felt a surge of love for her parents. The road ahead was difficult, but she wanted to walk a new path now, an honest one.

The sound of a scooter screeching to a halt outside the school gate interrupted her thoughts. It was Zafar. He looked dishevelled and frantic. He saw Mona and ran straight to her.

'I am so, so angry with myself for oversleeping! I just kept tossing and turning all night and then realized I had missed the alarm.' Zafar held her palm as he spoke.

It was Mona's turn to be calm. She reassured Zafar with a soft, gentle tone.

'I am just returning from the principal's office. A.P. called Mom and Dad too.' Mona couldn't believe she was not angry with Zafar for not showing up, but she really wasn't. In fact, she was glad she got the opportunity to find her own voice.

'Oh my God! I feel so, so guilty. I let you down, Mona. Listen, if you want to never speak to me again, I will understand. I just hope you don't hate me.' Zafar's voice trembled.

Their fingers intertwined.

'No, Zafar. I could never hate you. I know you didn't do this on purpose. I trust you with my life. Strangely enough, I am actually glad you didn't come on time. I surprised myself with the things I said and the strength with which I defended both of us today.

It sounds weird, but I feel proud of myself. I feel like a grown-up, for once!'

Wish we could hug each other right now, but one controversy a day is good enough.

They let go of each other's fingers slowly. There were classes that needed to be attended, unfortunately.

'Oh, and listen. Do you mind if I tag you in a story? Apparently, there is a photo of us doing the rounds.' Mona needed Zafar's permission.

'Do what you like. I trust you.' Zafar blew a kiss at her and ran off to his class.

*

Mona walked back to class and took her seat behind Paro, who looked at her and whispered, 'All okay?'

'Better than okay. Send me that photo during the break, Paro.'

Paro looked puzzled. 'What are you going to do?'

'Keep it close. At least someone took a photo of the two of us! I was too scared to.'

Paro looked at Mona like she had gone bananas, 'Can you just tell me what this is all about?'

Mona giggled. 'It's not a rumour. It's true! Zafar and I were together yesterday and guess what. It was the most bestest first date ever.'

'Most bestest isn't a word.' Paro rolled her eyes.

Mona told Paro all about her date during recess, eating mouthfuls of chowmein.

'Wow, Mona. That was some adventurous date!' Paro said, as she copied Mona's biology homework.

'The funny thing is, I told Zafar I wanted a fun story about my first date to tell my grandkids. Not a boring one. I think this story exceeds my expectations!'

'Eewww! Grandkids?? What if you don't have any? Maybe you should write about this.' Paro stuffed her face with the chowmein.

'Maybe I will. Someday,' she said, licking off the last bit of greasy noodles from Paro's tiffin box. 'Right now, however, I need to write to my troll.'

She uploaded the photo of Zafar and her on her Insta story. She tagged Zafar on it and wrote: 'Don't we look good together, Zafar, despite the poor photography skills? Do better next time, dear stalker.'

Zafar shared the story on his Gram almost immediately.

Mona smiled a Mona Lisa smile.

Happy New Year*

Nandana Dev Sen

'Hello, Didi?' I run into our bedroom and grab the phone that sits on the table between our beds. Didi went off to university a while ago, but her bed still has her patchwork kantha, just like mine. Ma had got the two blankets stitched for us using her old saris the year before she became a star. Our beds still smell of Ma.

'How did you know it was me?' I can hear my sister smile. She sounds so much like Ma, except when she sings. 'I'm just around the corner! Are you all packed? I should be there in one . . . two . . . no, exactly three minutes!'

'One, two, three! Ek, dui, teen . . . Bhooter Raja dilo bor!' I sing from *Goopy Gyne Bagha Byne*. Quite out of tune as always. I'm the one who turned out to be as tone-deaf as Ma, while Didi got Baba's deep Tagore-song voice.

---

* A story titled 'Happy New Year: A Short Story about Childhood Trauma' by Nandana Dev Sen, published in The Wire, 2017.

'Oof, that's ENOUGH!' laughs Didi. I can totally imagine her covering her ear with her free hand. Then, as if to say sorry, Didi hums a line too. '*Jobor-jobor teen bor, ek dui teen!*' Totally in tune, as always. She hangs up.

My favourite Satyajit Ray song seems pretty perfect right now, as I start packing my Dora suitcase. It does feel like I've got three blessings, though not from the King of Ghosts, like in the song. Well, at least two amazing, jobor-jobor blessings. Number One—Didi is coming home for dinner after a very long time. Number Two—we are going on a holiday together! Not terribly far, but I will be spending a whole week in the sunny seaside apartment that Didi and her best friend Rahnuma share. It's in a place called Seven Bungalows. They live in a very tall building, not much of a bungalow at all, but it has a lovely garden with orange swings soaring above the messy grey sea.

I really like Rahnuma, though when I first met her on Didi's twenty-first birthday this year, I thought she was a little scary. We had all gone to the white building where my grandmother lives with other older ladies. The first thing I noticed about Rahu was the Kaali on her forearm, flaunting a necklace of dead men's heads and a spikey blood-red tongue. Along with that fierce tattoo, Rahu had reddish hair broken into thick ropes of *jata*. But unlike Goddess Kaali, Rahu is not fierce at all. She has the biggest smile, and always smells of sandalwood. When our grandmother had offered to use a bottle of coconut oil and a bucket of *reetha* bubbles to rescue Rahu's matted hair, Didi had got quite upset. 'They are dreadlocks, Dimma, not jata, and her hair is perfectly clean!' she had cried, while Rahu simply smiled her calm, soft smile, without a word.

Can I tell you a secret? For a year now, Didi has been trying to take me away to stay over at her place. I'm thrilled that Baba has finally agreed, but I know that he only said yes after Didi had a proper fight with him about it on the phone. I know this because I was listening in from my room. 'I'm an adult now, Baba, and I am perfectly capable of looking after her.' Didi was saying this so firmly that she sounded almost angry. 'In fact, now that I'm twenty-one, I can even legally . . .' That's as far as she got because Baba slammed the phone down then. But she had won, because that night over dinner, Baba told me that I could spend the last week of my winter holidays with Didi.

Now, what's *not* a secret is how super excited I am! Didi's neighbourhood is not at all like where we live in Navy Nagar. Her road is lined with colourful cafes, ice-cream parlours, flower shops, pet-grooming salons and restaurants that stay open late and play all kinds of music. They even have karaoke nights! How awesome is that?

*

'Nikki!' Didi walks in briskly, her boy-cut hair (as Dimma calls it) glossy as always. 'Aren't you a bit too old for Dora? I must remember to get you a new case. Hey, have you packed your favourite books?'

'But I'm only going for a week!'

'Well . . . But what if you decide to stay longer?' Didi smiles. 'And better pack Ma's kanthas. Bombay can get quite cold in January.'

I add my *Asterix* omnibus, *Heidi* and *Abol Tabol* to the pile, and start folding the kanthas.

'Oh, and make sure you bring that album of Ma's photos too.'

'What?' I say, surprised. 'But it's so huge!'

'That's okay, it will be fun to go through it together, won't it?' Then she adds under her breath, 'Maybe it's time for Ma to get away from this house too . . .'

Her voice sounds a bit funny somehow, but when she catches me looking at her, Didi throws me one of her cheery winks.

'And don't forget to pack games and movies you like . . . Now, let me go sort out dinner like I promised I would.' She pops out of the room as quickly as she'd popped in.

Didi is right. I might as well take *Moana*, *Goopy Gyne* and *Inside Out* with me to her place, and UNO and snakes and ladders too. Those were Ma's favourite games, but Baba never plays with me anyway. In fact, he hardly watches any films or TV shows with me either. Sometimes we do watch *I Love Lucy* because Ma used to love it, but he never laughs out loud even when Lucy is so funny that my tummy feels like it's about to split. Come to think of it, Baba pretty much stopped smiling altogether, after Ma became a star. I guess he's just not the smiley kind. Ma used to tease him that he lost his sense of humour in Car-Gill.

I don't know what kind of a car that was, and why it made Baba all serious, but I suppose he did lose his sense of humour somewhere. I remember the time Didi dressed up in his three-piece suit for fun, and I wore my best party dress, the fluffy one handed down by Didi (which she had not even worn once)! It was a little too big for me still, but I loved it because it was blue, Ma's favourite colour. And it had lots of sparkly bits on it. Giggling together, Didi and I started waltzing around our room. That's when Baba had walked in. He was furious. 'You're not a boy, Sharmila!' he yelled, and poor Didi got a terrible thrashing that night. He has never beaten me that way. Maybe because I'm smaller?

But Baba doesn't hit Didi so hard anymore, not since she moved away. The last time it was really bad was when she refused to join the Indian Army like he wanted her to, so she could 'be respected in the world'.

'Girls are not even allowed to take the NDA exam, Baba—it just shows how little our military wants to respect its women!' she had cried. 'In any case, I never want to make a living from war.'

She'd rather be a practising journalist, she'd said, than get a Maha Vir Chakra like our father. Baba got so mad at Didi that night that I got very, very scared. I wished Ma had not become a star and could have calmed him down. Because when I tried to stop him, it just made him angrier and he slapped me too.

When Didi came back from the hospital that night with stitches on her lip, all Baba said was, 'If you decide to be a journalist, make sure you don't write anything against our government.'

'Always the patriot!' Didi had laughed strangely— an odd one-sided laugh because of her swollen lip— and had banged the door to our room shut. It was all terribly loud and angry and it made me feel very queasy. When Didi turned around and saw that I was ready to burst into tears all over again, her face cleared and she hugged me tight. She put on my best song, 'If you believe in fairies, clap your hands! Clap-clap-clap!' Then she picked up Ragini, my rag doll, and started clapping her floppy cloth hands together until I just had to smile.

Didi always knows how to make me feel better. In fact, she's been my most fun playmate for as long as I can remember, though she is twelve years older than me. Years ago, when Ma and I were making Ragini out of Dimma's old white sari, Didi had joined in happily, sticking one of Ma's big red bindis on the doll's tiny forehead. It had suddenly made my rag doll seem like a real person.

I carefully lay Ragini down in my suitcase. As I struggle to carry Ma's heavy photo album towards Dora, I stub my toe against the foot of the bed. Ouch! Why did I have to be so clumsy? I mean, Ma was such a graceful dancer after all, with all those prizes that I keep lined up on our shelf! But then again, I guess Ma could be a little klutzy too, just like me. I remember she would keep getting hurt from falling over and banging into walls and things. And it never happened when we were with her, so Didi and I couldn't even help! She'd have new bruises and cuts in the morning and when I touched them anxiously, she'd smile and say, 'It's okay, Nikki shona. I fell again, that's all.'

*

Dimma told us that Ma had loved performing on stage since her childhood, but she stopped dancing when she married Baba. In fact, this big album is full of pictures of her dance shows, with Ma looking like a goddess in her Odissi costume. I never saw her onstage, but I remember how Ma would pick me up in her arms and dance around our house, singing fully off-key as always, red bindi flashing on her forehead. Her laughter would spill like sunshine into every corner of our big blue house. She burst into the living room one day with all that light and warmth while I was watching *Frozen* on TV.

'I've just been to the hospital,' Ma sang, 'and I have the best news in the whole world! You girls are going to have a baby sister!'

'Nandini! We promised the doctor you'd be quiet about this.' Baba had walked in behind her, not looking at all as happy as Ma. 'And there's no need to discuss this with the children until we've talked.'

I don't know what they talked about that night, though I could hear some shouting about boys and the army and having two girls at home already. The next morning, Baba drove Ma to the hospital again. She was gone just a couple of hours, but in the next few weeks, Ma was never the same again. No more ripples of laughter. No more bouncing around the house. No more singing out of tune. Instead, we'd hear Baba and Ma scream at each other late into the night. Didi and I would hold hands tightly as my tummy got all knotted up inside. We tried to vanish under our kanthas, our stretched-out arms making a bridge between our twin beds.

As I zip up my Dora case, a gust of wind slams the window shut. I get up to close it properly. The night sky glitters with billions of stars. Which one is Ma, I wonder?

Everything changed a year ago, when I was eight. It was 31 December. A busy day for me as I was going to the year-end picnic with my class, then Dimma would pick me up for the night. Ma and Baba were going to the Army Ball, while Didi would go out with her friends. As I rushed out to catch the school bus that morning, I heard Baba and Ma having one of their extra-loud fights, the kind that made my tummy feel all weird. I think Ma was saying that she was feeling too tired to go to the ball. Later that day, as I was stepping out of the bus, I saw Didi running towards me with tears streaming down her face. She grabbed my hand and dragged me home, running at full speed. There was a crowd outside our house, an ambulance waiting. Strangers were carrying an odd shape out on a stretcher. It looked like a body wrapped in a white sheet from head to toe, with a big round patch of red right in the middle of the covered head. As if my rag doll had secretly grown into a giant, and Ma's bindi had somehow melted and spread all over it.

Baba was standing at the door in total silence, looking stunned. Before I understood anything, Dimma wrapped us up in her arms, her body shaking with sobs. 'Your mother has become a star now,' she said to us in a broken voice, choking.

*

'Dinner is ready!' Didi calls out from the dining room. Baba is watching the news, like he always does during dinner. The headlines crackle loudly as I sit down to eat.

'Gun violence is disturbingly on the rise across the globe. In the first twenty-four hours of the new year, 210 separate incidents of gun violence have happened across the United States. At least sixty-four people were killed . . .'

I wish he'd switch it off. I don't mind hearing the news every night while we eat, but it would be so nice for us to just talk sometimes. As it is, the three of us never have meals together any more.

'The victims included a one-year-old, several teenagers and a mother and daughter. A troubling statistic to add to the thirty-nine killed in Istanbul on New Year's Eve . . .'

Baba mutes the TV—thank God—as Didi ladles dal on to my rice. 'It's a shame that they let anybody have a gun in America,' he says. 'Only responsible parties like the police or the military should be allowed to bear arms, just like it is here in India.'

Didi stops serving and stares at Baba, as dal drips in big yellow drops all over our starched white tablecloth.

'America should definitely be tougher on gun control, Baba, but India has the second highest number of murders in the world every year.' Didi fills Baba's bowl. 'We never speak about everyday violence here, that's all. And the youth are most at risk, in fact.'

'Young people get into fights everywhere in the world, but at least we are safe from gun violence, Sharmila. Our gun laws are tight, and the report of the National Crime Records Bureau shows that—'

'Actually, that report shows that close to 3700 people were murdered with guns in India in just one year,' Didi cuts him off. 'And more than 85 per cent were killed by unlicensed arms. So, how safe are we?'

'Don't you dare talk back at me!' snaps Baba, pushing his chair back and getting up angrily.

Oh no, please God, no . . . It's getting all loud and horrible again . . . Like it used to be between Ma and Baba.

'Calm down, Baba,' says Didi. 'I'm doing an assignment on that NCRB report you're talking about, and we are just having a conversation, aren't we? There's no reason to get cross.'

'Why do you always have to disagree with everything I say?' Baba's voice gets louder.

I get that panicky feeling in my tummy again as my heart starts pounding super fast. I have to make it all go quiet again somehow. I have to say something. Right away.

'Please don't be angry, Baba,' I blurt out. 'I'm sure Ma would not want that if she was here!'

'But she isn't here, Nikasha, is she?' Baba hisses. 'You know that your ma is a star now, so why don't you just keep her out of this!'

'She isn't a star, Baba,' I hear Didi say. 'She is dead. From a gunshot.'

'She died in an accident!' Baba cries out.

'She died from a bullet,' Didi says quietly.

It happened while Ma was cleaning Baba's gun. I'd never seen Ma clean a gun before, so I'm sure she wasn't very good at it and I wish she had never tried to do it. When the gun went off, Baba had rushed in and taken it from her, but it was too late. The neighbours had found him like that, gun in hand, frozen in shock. The police had been very understanding, of course. Baba was a hero, after all, he even had a Maha Vir Chakra.

'A bullet from a gun that should have never been on your desk,' Didi's voice continues, soft but firm. 'A gun you brought into the home of two children, and a woman suffering from . . .'

What is Didi saying? Ma didn't mean to shoot herself, did she? It was an accident, of course . . . wasn't it? As my thoughts get all tangled up around each other, I hear Didi's words echo from what seems like another universe.

'Will you ever tell us what really happened that day, Baba?'

Baba's face looks like the darkest storm as he swoops down and yanks Didi off her chair.

'Enough!' Didi catches his hands and holds them in mid-air, her grip so tight that her knuckles seem to be bursting through her skin.

They stare at each other, hands shaking, eyes full of anger and hurt, for what seems like the scariest forever. I'm about to throw up.

Then a car honks outside. Rahu's code, three short hoots.

Didi lets go of Baba's hands. He sits back in his chair, suddenly looking very old. Without another word, Didi picks up my case and takes my hand. 'Say goodbye, Nikki,' she whispers, almost to herself, as we walk out.

Rahnuma is waiting outside. 'Is that all?' Rahu asks as she puts Dora into the boot. 'Do you have everything you will need, Nikki?'

'Yes,' I say slowly, climbing into the back seat. I'm so glad I packed Ma's kanthas and her photo album. 'I have everything.'

Didi puts my seat belt on and turns back to look at our house. I can see her eyes get shiny with tears.

I haven't seen Didi cry in a long time. In fact, I haven't seen her cry since Ma had become a . . . a . . . Since Ma had become dead.

Didi gets into the front seat. Rahu holds Didi's hand for a moment, then starts the car.

'Happy New Year, Nikki,' says Rahu. I can feel her sandalwood smell all around me, warm and sweet, like a hug.

'Happy New Year, Ma,' I say softly to myself, as I watch our big blue house vanish around the corner.

To All the Boys We've Failed Before

(AKA 7 Lies We Tell Boys for Them to Become 'Men')

Nikhil Taneja

Dear boys,
I write this letter to you as someone who used to be you.

Yes, it does sound weird when someone who isn't your dad says this, but I was once a teenager myself. I don't know if Charles Dickens was inspired by puberty when he wrote, 'It was the best of times, it was the worst of times.' But to me, it seems like a fairly accurate description of *teenagehood*.

Like all teenagers, I was absolutely sure about everything I knew of the world while also being completely clueless about who I was and what my place in it would be. I had elaborate plans of exactly how my life would pan out over the next thirty years while also not being sure what the very next day had in store for me. I sincerely believed everything would work itself out as soon as you became an adult, but I silently feared everything will come crashing down the second someone found out you aren't ready to be one. Of course, I never let the fear hold me back; in fact, I never, *ever*, spoke about the fear at all. Because boys are not afraid.

I'm sorry to be the one to break this to you through this dorky letter, but that's a lie.

Not a lie that I'm telling you (I just wrote some fairly emo stuff right at the top), but a lie that was told to me, and a lie that is probably being told to you at this very moment, by your well-meaning father who was told this too, or by your always-*extra* mother who wants you to 'toughen up', or by your school 'bro' or your college 'bhai' who seems to know what he's doing better than you do, even though he doesn't seem to be doing much at all. They don't *mean* to lie to you. It's just that they genuinely believe that to be the truth . . . most of them do anyway. Just like they believe that most girls are weak.

That one's a lie too. And so is the one about boys being macho and strong and tough and wearers of the colour blue, and of girls being the 'opposite' of it all.

There is no space within the confines of these clichés for young people to be their own *selves*, for those who are exhausted from the pressure of living up to them, for those who don't just fall within these gendered categories but are proud to be outside of them, for those who are trying to break away from that body that knows it is very different.

I was once a boy who also believed in these lies and then some.

And as a ~~man~~ human being who has had some time to fight them, escape them and refute them, and is still doing so, I'm going to tell you about each of these lies in detail today. So that you have the choice to be the kind of ~~man~~ human being you'd like to become.

#7 Boys need to have a plan

I always loved plans growing up. I was the boy who would write in his own slam book(s) first, before giving it to my friends (read: crush), because I loved putting down all my ambitions and goals and life missions on paper, and longingly looking at them in my spare time. I was always pretty good at being good: I did well at school, I got lots of certificates in extracurricular activities, I turned down a girl who asked me out because I didn't want to 'betray my parents' (true story), and I studied science in high school and engineering in college because what else would I study? Arts? LOL.

The thing is, I did want to explore the arts. I just didn't know it was even an option. Because it was really important for me to 'stick to the plan'. I was a boy and that's what boys have to do in order to be called successful men: boys *need* to get a *safe* degree that buys them a *decent* house, so they can get themselves a *lovely* wife and eventually, a *settled* life. And every boy is judged on, and defined by, his ability in reaching this final milestone of 'settling down' in his young adult life—the way Frodo's journey was defined by casting the One Ring into the fires of Mount Doom, or to put it in a 2021 analogy, the way influencers are judged on being able to get a paid 'collab' in their Instagram DMs.

I followed this 'plan' for a long time, only to be diagnosed with clinical anxiety one day—because I was living the story that was handed to me by someone else.

Because 'settle', according to society, is supposed to mean 'successful', but it is, I realized, another word for 'compromise'. A compromise some boys make when they want to be writers or YouTubers or start-up founders or stylists, but end up taking engineering and medicine and law and finance because they are *safe*. A compromise some boys make by spending the first few years of their careers in joyless jobs to 'save for the future', even if they aren't happy with their present. A compromise that some boys make by getting married straight out of college, first job in hand, because they have been told their job is to 'take care of their family' even if they haven't yet learnt to take care of themselves. And what of the boys who compromise on their very identities to fit into a way of life that's heteronormative, because 'that' is not part of the plan for them just because they weren't born the 'boys' their parents thought them to be?

Dear boys, don't 'settle' and don't *ever* compromise.

#6 Boys have to be the man of the house

Every boy growing up in India has a mythical, mystical, fantastical and utopian creature they have been compared to all their lives. This creature, the ideal boy, is called 'Sharmaji ka beta' (Sharmaji's son). Your personal Sharmaji ka beta could be your neighbour's son, a cousin, the class topper, the school topper, the district topper or the boy whose mugshot is featured on a billboard that declares him a life topper (because he cracked *the* entrance exam) but who looks like he hasn't slept (or bathed) since he hit puberty. The problem is not that this boy exists; the problem is that since he exists, you must now be him.

The assumption is that boys *have* to be the 'man of the house' one day and carry the legacy of the family name forward. It starts from the day the cries of 'Badhai ho, ladka hua hai' (Congratulations, it's a son) are sounded, not as good wishes but as a victory lap. This legacy becomes a lifelong responsibility (and never a burden) that boys have to fulfil with pride, honour and no complaints whatsoever. Because if they don't, they will be reminded of Sharmaji ka beta, who not only does all of this as well as Virat Kohli bats or Pankaj Tripathi acts (or Ravish Kumar facts?) but is also a great <insert whatever they need you to be that day>, or at least better than you can ever be.

And if a boy, tired of constantly being reminded of his inadequacies, ever wonders out loud why he should be like somebody else when he can simply be like himself, he will be instructed by his parents to respect his elders and basically, to just shut up. Because they were told the same lies by their parents growing up—that only the old are worthy of respect and the young are to follow, agree, obey, acquiesce and never question because 'that is the way the world works'. They believed this because they had no reason to believe otherwise, most didn't have the access or opportunities we did, so why can't we be the same as them?

Dear boys, remember, you don't have to follow in the footsteps of the boys before you.

#5 Boys can't have hobbies

I started writing at a very early age. From journals to diaries to the aforementioned slam books, to short stories and film scripts and books that never were to be, I would find refuge in words whenever I had thoughts in my head and feelings in my heart. At fourteen, I started getting published in a youth magazine in Bahrain, and before I graduated from school, I had a weekly column and had interviewed the likes of Shankar Mahadevan, Mohanlal, Junoon (the band) and even Michael Schumacher!

But much like it was for Farhan in *3 Idiots*, engineering had been pre-decided for me simply because I was a boy. And as the only idiot in my life, I set it in stone in my own head after a conversation I had with my parents at the age of sixteen, where my writing was dismissed not as a possible career but as a 'hobby' and I was explained that there is a caste system for streams in our country too, and a boy's success, and how he'll be treated in life, depends on the stream he takes in college.

If he is intelligent (aka gets 90 per cent and above), he has to take science and engineering.

If he is average (aka gets 70 per cent and above), he takes commerce.

But Heaven forbid, if he is a failure (aka anything below 70 per cent), he is condemned to arts.

It was then very obvious to me that I had to do engineering, since my marks proved that I was intelligent, and as a boy, being successful in life was my overarching goal since birth. So I didn't take arts after school, and a four-year-long, parent-approved engineering degree later, I went ahead and did what I wanted anyway . . . the arts. I turned my hobby into a career, and a *kinda, sorta* successful one too, if I may humblebrag a bit.

In a time before Chetan Bhagat and his first book existed, I couldn't have known this at all. In fact, I was just happy that I could pursue writing as a hobby, because a lot of the boys I knew didn't even get that opportunity! Yes, my friends played sports, and sometimes, they'd read and write and paint and dance and dream, but all of that was 'allowed' only so that they could get trophies at school, which would be seen as one more shining star on their shining CVs. Any hobby without an immediate or foreseeable reward was deemed a 'waste of time'.

A boy's worth is often measured in the marks he gets at school, and where he spends his time every single day growing up is a function of how much it will contribute directly and inevitably to the 'package' he gets in his job as a grown up. Anything off the beaten path is seen as an abject failure.

Dear boys, you are more than your marks.

#4 Boys can't fail

A few years ago, when I turned thirty, I was diagnosed with clinical anxiety. It was at a time when I was, any way you look at it (and especially if you looked at my social feeds), 'settled' and I considered going to therapy—as a man, it was a personal failure. It meant that I had somehow turned out broken, where other men remained strong, and therapy proved that I was a lesser man than all these other men.

But prioritizing my mental health and taking my anxiety seriously changed my life. It made me realize how absolutely, completely, enormously stupid I was to think that it would somehow make me 'weak'. It helped me break all these ridiculous stereotypes in my head about what men can and cannot do, and what a man should and should not be. But it also helped me recognize that all of my issues, as varied as they may be, had one thing in common: that I couldn't cope with the idea of having failed.

I grew up believing that boys are meant to succeed because it is the mission statement of their lives, and that boys who fail are social outcasts and have no place in society. Because in failing at one insignificant thing, they have failed at the most important thing of all: in fulfilling their purpose as a boy.

Boys are not only fed this untruth at home by their parents but also at school by their teachers, who put tremendous pressure on them to succeed while never providing them with any support system if they don't. This may be triggering for some to read, but India has the highest rate of student suicides in the world, with one student suicide every hour and a majority of them boys (a ratio of almost 3 to 1). What use is an education system that gives students degrees, but not the tools and resources to understand and deal with mental health?

What use is an education system that turns studying into a game, and where entrance exams are literally called 'competition' in which you either win or lose?

What use is an education system that places such a high priority on these arbitrary distinctions that it gives students the impression that passing them will not only determine the course of their lives, but also whether even to live?

Dear boys, you have to be okay with failure.

#3 Boys don't feel pain

Ever wondered why the Indian film industry, despite being one of the most prolific film industries in the entire world, does not have too many superhero films? I think it's because every Indian film is really a superhero film anyway. Think about it. In our films, the male lead is called a 'hero' and the female lead is called a 'heroine'. The 'hero' is traditionally a tall, handsome, fair, heterosexual, muscular man whose job is to save the world, save the day and save the girl. The heroine is traditionally a tall, beautiful, fair, heterosexual, shapely woman whose job is to dance, over and over again, and wait until the hero saves her. Indian films have never needed a superhero because Indian films have Salman Khan. And Rajinikanth. And Akshay Kumar. And 'Thalapathy' Vijay. And of course, the OG 'Angry Young Man', Amitabh Bachchan.

Generations of boys who grew up watching Indian blockbusters were told *'mard ko dard nahin hota'* (boys don't feel pain). They started believing that they had to grow up to be the 'hero' who didn't feel any pain, while many girls, unfortunately, started believing that they have to wait for a 'hero' to save them from theirs.

Until the recent arrival of the Ayushmann Khurranas and Fahadh Faasils, the only Indian men who felt—and romanticized—pain did so primarily because they had trouble understanding consent or boundaries. Because to be a 'hero', you have to be ever-strong, and ever-undefeated. So pain wasn't an option. And rejection was even worse because *'ladkiyon ki na mein haan hai'* (for girls, 'no' means 'yes'). Our screen heroes have always been the supreme defenders and protectors of womenkind—not because they needed heroes, but because boys have always been told this is their 'duty'.

Here's the thing: every boy feels pain, but most boys don't talk about it. Instead, we bury it deep inside our hearts under the garb of mard ko dard nahin hota, even believing that we are the only ones going through it. And one day, we crash and crack and break down, often becoming violent and abusive towards those who give us pain. Empathy is seen as a sign of weakness, and the highest form of this weakness is empathy for ourselves. One that allows us to accept that sometimes we don't need to be heroes and sometimes we don't have to be strong and sometimes people will be unkind and sometimes life won't be fair and sometimes we will be rejected.

Dear boys, allow yourself this pain.

#2 Boys are born to be treated like royalty

If Indian movies deem the Indian man a 'hero', Indian mothers deem the Indian boy something even grander. Boys are not just boys, they are a gift from the gods, they are the scions of the family, they are the fulfilment of her destiny as a woman, they are the brightest stars in the entire galaxy, they are straight outta royalty, they are . . . *drum rolls* . . . 'raja beta'. A prince, no less.

And while the raja beta is still compared to *Sharmaji ka raja beta* and pressurized to do all the things boys must do, if he does the things expected of him exceedingly well, he is given the greatest leeway, even wider than the leeway Indian parents give the forwards they read on WhatsApp. The raja beta is fed, clothed, sheltered, protected and treated as magnificently and royally as his parents can afford to, so long as he becomes the man they want him to be. Choice or free will is only for lesser mortals. The duty to prove his raja-ness is sacrosanct, and that's what he is trained for all his life, much like Arjun was trained to be a warrior and Arya Stark was trained to whoop all Valars in her way. And every time he doesn't perform up to the mark, the ceaseless tap of the gifts that were once showered upon him is closed until further notice. Legend has it that in a few tragic and devastating cases, gifts are also known to be revoked and taken away forever—I still miss my Walkman from 2004!

The problem with this quid pro quo is that, like any other addiction, the royal treatment is a dopamine hit that every boy's brain is conditioned to be addicted to. And the boys who find themselves at the top of the food chain start believing that this treatment should be extended to them outside of their homes as well. That every living being who crosses their paths and every woman they believe is 'worthy' of their affection should show them the respect that they undeniably deserve or they will just have no choice but to snatch it, in any way they can. And since the dawn of time, society has excused this behaviour and resolutely looked away because 'boys will be boys'.

And so, toxic geniuses, from Steve Jobs to Joss Whedon (Yes, I went there!), and everyone else in between, are worshipped and celebrated despite their documented aggression and abuse in the workplaces. Most of the world quietly looks the other way as men do what 'men must do'. This rotten behaviour has long existed under the very roofs many of us are born; our fathers or grandfathers or uncles have been allowed to treat our mothers or sisters or any other female members around them with anger, violence, abuse or contempt, only because they are men, and only because they were told growing up that as long as they make money, they can get away with anything.

Even the ones who are kinder are kind only within the limitations of the gendered roles they believe they must fit in, and so they seldom cook, clean, wash dishes or clothes, or split the labour in the house in any meaningful way because that's not their 'department'. And the ones that do help around must be thanked and showered with gratitude for going out of their way to not be 'those men'.

Dear boys, it's time to reject those toxic gender norms.

#1 Boys must be men

Actually, that's not a total lie. Some day, boys are going to be men. But you don't have to be the kind of man society wants you to be, or even a man at all. Because just like there is no one kind of a boy, there is also no one kind of a man. You can and should be any kind of person you want to be, anyone who says otherwise is lying to you.

A settled life does not have to be a compromised one; it can be a life that you settle into, by doing the things that bring you peace, by finding the people who bring you joy, by making the mistakes that bring you experience and by living in a way that makes you feel alive. You can and you should find your truth before you make a 'plan', without taking on the burden of the boys who came before you.

It isn't going to be easy to find your own path, but when you think of it, perhaps the first-ever Sharmaji ka beta, generations ago, became the gold standard of boys because he too forged a path so unique that everyone was then asked to follow his. Perhaps you are born not to fit in, but to stand out and it may be your hobby that gets you there, even if there are a few failures along the way.

Each of us have failed at most things before succeeding at something. But the goalposts to success keep changing, the standards of success are arbitrary and there are never enough things to achieve. Success doesn't always guarantee happiness but failure will always gift you perspective, even if it comes with a little pain.

Pain doesn't need to be overcome, only processed. So ask for the help you need. You will not get cookies for being 'strong' and you certainly won't get any for thinking of women as 'weak'. Remember these two things. One, that life doesn't owe any of us anything. And two, that you will have your heart broken and you can't expect differently. Life will not give you any royal treatment because you are a boy, even if your parents will.

The things that make a boy special are the things that make any human special—their love, empathy, honesty, character and the dignity with which they lead their lives. The moment we believe that people from any other gender are any different from us solely because of their identity, or solely because of ours, is the day we let every other lie told to us become gospel.

Because, dear boys, instead of trying to get away with saying 'boys will be boys', it is up to you to hold both yourself and other boys accountable and push us all to do better. To believe that that's just how 'men' are is to excuse the toxicity of the society that has led to men who think they're better than you and me and anyone else.

So, in the limited time we all have, strive to be kinder, empower others with empathy and create safe spaces to express yourself. But mainly, listen to anyone else who seeks it. Go on to be the man you know how to be, the man you want to be, the man you hoped to be.

Because believing that such a society isn't possible is only a lie you will be telling yourself.

Love,
Nikhil

A Bird Called Freedom*

Hannah Lalhlanpuii

My life has always been defined by simplicity. I do not know of a world outside my small town of Aizawl except the ones we read about in school. Busy streets, markets bustling with people, cars honking . . . I have no idea how to picture any town with such commotion because mine was quiet, calm and peaceful.

With half-open eyes, I stare at the red-winged blackbird perched on the windowsill. Grandfather must have opened my window when he woke up. I sit up with great difficulty and place my feet on the wooden floor with a loud thud. The bird leaves immediately, probably to wake another sleepy kid up.

I look out at the mist-covered hills in the distance through the window and wonder what snow feels like. Our teachers often talk about the snow-covered

---

* Excerpt from Hannah's upcoming book *When Blackbirds Fly* (Duckbill Books, 2022)

streets in London and Paris, and I can imagine myself
running as snow falls. Sometimes I wonder if the thin
white clouds that cover the hills and valleys here can
be rolled up into tiny pieces to create snowfall. The
smell of freshly brewed tea wakes me up from these
lazy morning thoughts and I head towards the kitchen
where I pour myself some tea and grab a large chunk
of jaggery.

Grandfather's spot near the window is empty, he
must have gone on his usual rounds to the neighbouring
houses. I can hear Nu Thangi, the woman next door,
busying herself in the pigsty in their backyard. 'Eat up,
eat up. Here, come here.' Her voice is pitchy and shrill.
I often complain to Father about the awful stench
coming from the sty, which is always followed by his
short lecture on tolerance and keeping a broad mind.
Then I end up pacifying myself thinking of the good
share of pork we always get whenever they kill their
pigs for the meat.

After a quick meal, I walk to school with Father
marching beside me. Rini is not here today. I am
too tired to greet the sun and so, I stare down at my
freshly polished shoes, trying to keep them clean at
least until recess. Father accompanies me till we pass
by his school and I say goodbye to him. I spot Zuala
and his father on the other side of the road. I can tell
from the way they are dressed that they are headed to

his grandparents' farm. Zuala has a haircut that looks as though someone simply put a bowl on his head and slashed out whatever popped out. He and I have been friends ever since I can remember. He had dropped out from school after he finished his middle school as his parents needed him to work on the family farm. Zuala's house is located on the peak of Tuikhuahtlang, a locality right next to ours, on a hillock. Every weekend, we would spend the entire day playing with wooden cartwheels and listening to his uncle talk. His uncle is an outgoing guy, a pleasant character as far as I can tell, and we really look up to him. He joined the Mizo National Front (MNF) two years ago and since then I have barely seen him. In our current situation, joining the MNF meant wearing the mark of a rebel and it became a big deal among the young men to dare each other to join the movement. There were times when I thought Zuala's uncle was dead and then he would suddenly reappear out of the blue and then disappear again just as abruptly.

'Off to the farm?' I ask Zuala, squinting across the sun's heat.

'It's already time for *mangkhawh*. We have to burn the ground for new plantations,' he replies, also trying to adjust his eyes to the morning sun.

'Why don't you come with us? We'll be back before sunset,' says Pa Hmuaka, Zuala's father, as he adjusts the strap of the big dirty cloth bag hanging from his shoulder. It amazes me how different fathers can be.

It is a tempting offer, not only because of my ill-fated, excessive loathing for school but also because I have been to their farmhouse quite a few times and it was the ideal getaway.

'Father won't be happy about it. You know how he hates me skipping school,' I say with a scowl on my face.

'Then next time, huh?'

'All right, see you then. Don't set yourself on fire,' I say and walk on.

Many a times, I have felt jealous of Zuala's lifestyle. He doesn't have to go to school and burning down trees sounds so much more fun than sitting in class and listening to teachers all day long. The walk home with Rini is always the only highlight of my day. Now, walking to school alone feels like one of those mundane tasks that rarely brings with it anything to talk about. It is somewhat like brushing your teeth or washing your face in the morning. You get to it and your brain somehow automatically discards the memory into some obscure part of your brain, never to be found again. As I walk past the majestic banyan tree standing tall in the middle of Aizawl Treasury Square, I stop to look up at the huge brown branches stretching out as if they are about to hug the sky and I wonder if Rini's squirrel might be dead. It's a daily ritual for me and Rini to stop at the banyan tree on our way back from school to feed the family of squirrels who have been dominating the majestic tree since we were kids. We have named the squirrels we call our own. The one I called 'mine' was so ordinary that it had no identification marks and I could not tell it apart from the others. So I gave up on it unlike Rini, whose squirrel's pelt is fluffier than all the others. Her squirrel has been missing for almost a week.

I reach school as the second bell rings. I hurriedly join the others who have already lined up for the morning school assembly and my eyes fly straight to the spot where Rini stands. I breathe a sigh of relief the moment my stretched neck allows me to see her neatly plaited hair amidst the many black heads which I have absolutely no interest in. I hear the school headmistress Pi Sangpuii announce something about someone's death.

'Remember the kid?' Thana, the boy behind me asks in a whisper, too loud for my dreamy state that it makes me jump.

'Quiet,' I reply, refusing to take my eyes off Rini.

'Didn't you hear? He died yesterday.'

'Who died?' I ask, eager to end the unwanted conversation.

'That kid. The one whose cartridges we stole last week. Remember?'

'Oh, yes. I remember.'

Rini looks sad and shifts her feet back and forth.

'He died in a landslide. They said he was collecting leftover cartridges from the army trench yesterday in the evening. It rained suddenly and he got stuck in the landslide. Scary, huh?' Thana's morning breath smells like a rotten cabbage.

'Silence!' the shrill voice of the headmistress booms across the assembly. That, followed by the feedback of the speakers, leaves my heart pounding. Luckily, we aren't the only ones whispering, so no one looks at us, much to my relief. 'From now on, I would like to advise everyone to go straight home after school as you are all aware of the current situation. Do not roam the streets at night, especially without adults,' she says, before dismissing us. We all walk in a single file to our respective classrooms, like little black ants heading out for a day's hard work. I march uncomfortably close to the boy in front of me, who casts an uneasy glance at me.

The moment we enter the classroom everyone starts to talk about the boy who died in the landslide. Some of the girls look like they are close to tears, saying things like, 'I feel so bad for his parents', 'He was such a friendly kid', 'He once brought me oranges from their farm', 'We walked home together once'. Maybe that's what death does, making people feel like they used to be really close. I sit in my usual corner and think about the day we stole his cartridges. I didn't feel guilty back then, but the more I think about it, the more I hate myself for what we had done. I have nothing to say of him like my classmates do, about how close we used to be. The only connection I can make between him and me is that I stole something that belongs to him. 'Thou shall not steal.' I remember learning the Ten Commandments in Sunday school a year ago. If only we knew when people are going to meet their end, but I don't really know if that would make anything better or worse.

The history teacher comes in and we observe a moment of silence for the deceased, and the day goes on as usual. I try my best to act as if no one had died and I sit there, forcing my head to think about Rini, the banyan tree and the squirrels.

After the last bell, I stand awkwardly near the school water tank waiting for Rini to finish her sweeping duty. I can see Mr Sangthuama, our mathematics teacher engaged in a serious talk with Miss Engmawii, our English teacher who is admired by all the students not only because of her pretty round face but because she can speak English, which sounded a bit like the English missionaries. Maybe Mr Sangthuama is also secretly in love with her, or maybe he just admires her. But from the look on his face, I am pretty sure that he likes her, or her voice, whichever. Watching them talk, I feel a strange connection with the mathematics teacher, like we were both suppressing our feelings towards the girls we loved. Suddenly, I feel stupid about it. Then, I see Rini walking out from her classroom and a thought suddenly crosses my mind—what if the fact that I like her has been written all over my face all this time and she was just pretending to not know about it because we have been friends for so long? I look at Mr Sangthuama who did not know how obvious he was being; could I be the same?

Before I could think of other possible reasons as to why she might have ignored the signs on my face, she is already standing next to me.

'It's funny that you're never early for school and always too early to go home,' she says and gives me a smile with her eyes half-closed.

'And you do just the opposite?'

'Well, today's our sweeping duty so I couldn't leave early.'

The girls from her class walk past us and wave at us. I notice that some of them are giggling and whispering.

'Don't mind them. They think you're my boyfriend, but I've already told them that we're more like siblings.'

I cannot tell if I am happy or sad about what she just said. More of the latter, I suppose. Maybe she does not see me the way I see her, or maybe I am not presenting myself as the type of boy who would make a good boyfriend. I am almost ready to tell her how I really feel, but after what she just said, all my plans and preparations have gone down the drain. As we walk down the school hill, I cannot think of anything else.

'Hey, are you even listening?' she says with a raised voice and I realize I had missed whatever she said prior to that.

'Yes. I am listening,' I mumble.

'You look disturbed. Something bad happened today?'

'No, it's just . . . that kid who died. We stole his cartridges last week and I'm feeling pretty bad about it now that he's dead. That's all,' I lie.

'Oh, that's a good reason to feel bad. You know, the best thing is to do good for other people as much as you can. You never know when they'll leave, never giving you a chance to say sorry again,' she says, like an elder sister. Maybe she's right, we're more like siblings.

What she said makes me wonder if telling her about my feelings can be counted as 'doing good' to her or making her life worse. Like everyone else, I cannot tell when she or I will vanish from each other's life. I quickly try to get rid of the negative thoughts in my head and bring myself back to the moment.

'So, I think independence is just what we need right now, don't you think?' Rini goes on. It's surprising how she can jump from one topic to another.

'Oh, yes. You're right,' I try to follow suit.

'But my mother said that it won't be an easy thing to earn, the independence. Even if the MNF succeeded in bringing about independence, she said we'd have to struggle for years to stand on our own feet. But you know what I think? That is what every state had faced before. Even India itself was in a mess during the first five years after the British left.'

I have my hands in my pocket and she is playing with the ends of her braids as she talks. I cannot find any significant thought or idea to add to what she had just said. 'Independence' itself is too much of a mouthful for me. The talk about Mizoram fighting for self-government has been her obsession for the past three weeks. In fact, it is the talk of the town, and of the school. As for me, I am barely concerned about what is happening. Somehow, I am fed up with all the talk about independence, the soldiers and everything. Father walking around the house, listening to Rini talk, sitting with Grandfather by the window at night—life is perfect for me this way. My world is small, but I am free in it. I am independent and that's all that matters.

*

Grandfather smokes his pipe while I wash the dinner dishes at the sink, standing on a short stool. Even though he does not say it out loud, I can feel the sense of contentment he feels when blowing out long trains of smoke through the window. The house is quiet as usual. Father had gone out to pay a visit to one of his sick colleagues from our locality.

'Pu, what will be the story tonight?' I ask him, returning the dishes to their places.

'Well, that depends on the kind of story you're prepared to listen to,' he says, like some mysterious soothsayer, his crossed leg dangling like a child. As I put in the last steel bowl, I drop it and it hits the floor with a loud clanging sound, doing that thing steel bowls do when they're dropped on the floor—rolling about for hours until finally relaxing into an echoing last shriek.

'Careful, careful,' Grandfather shouts, doing that thing adults do after the mistake is made.

I am just done washing the plates when I hear a whistle outside. I can tell right away that it is Zuala, from the amount of spit muffling the sound. The whistling thing is like a ritual he always does before entering our door. He had been practising this 'ceremony' for as long as I can remember us being friends. Before I can turn to the door, Zuala enters ungreeted as usual, with a big bundle on his shoulder.

'Finished your dinner?' he says as he lays the bundle on the floor.

'Yes, I was just cleaning up. What's this for?' I ask.

'Well, we came back from the farm sooner than we planned. On our way home, we got lucky and got a whole lot of these bamboo shoots. Mother asked me to give you a share,' he says all out of breath, wiping the sweat off his brows and revealing said bamboo shoots.

'Those are some tasty-looking shoots you got there, Zuala,' says Grandfather, stretching his neck, 'but you shouldn't have risked coming here. The streets nowadays are unsafe after dark.'

'Yes, Pu. We got really lucky. I must be stinking. Haven't even taken a bath,' he says and pulls out the wooden stool from below the dining table.

'You should've come today. It was tiring but really fun,' he says.

'You cannot imagine how badly I wanted to come. Schools will probably be closed in a few days. Oh, by the way, remember the boy from school I told you about? The one whose cartridges I stole with my classmate. Remember?'

'Yes, you told me that last week,' says Zuala. I can hear the lack of curiosity in his voice, which almost makes me upset.

'Yes, that kid. He died yesterday in a landslide,' I say flatly as I take some of the bamboo shoots and place them on the kitchen table.

His eyes expand into big circles. 'What? He's dead? That's really unfortunate. It rained pretty hard in the evening yesterday,' he says, tying a knot on the bundle.

'Now, you two better be really careful. These things can happen to anyone,' says Grandfather, his voice heavy with a note of concern, always ready to join our conversations.

'Oh, I almost forgot to tell you. Uncle told me that they had another firing at the same spot last week. We should go there before the other boys dig out all the good ones,' Zuala says, lowering his voice.

Zuala and I have our own special collection of used cartridges that we keep in an empty ghee can. There is no prize or reward for it, but the cartridge collection has created a tough competition among boys of our age and news about who has the largest collection travels fast. The 'spot' that Zuala mentioned was a small mound on MacDonald Hill, just a stone's throw away from our school. It was a trench dugout used by the Indian Army to shoot at the rebels. We really don't care who shoots whom, as long as they leave behind the empty shells.

'But the headmaster has strictly banned us from going near the site after this fatal accident. They said the land slid down and covered him up like a corpse even before he died,' I say, bringing my palms together and grinding them together as if that would do anything.

'What was our last count?' Zuala asks, paying no attention to what I just said.

'Seventy-three when I counted last week.'

'We'll be able to have a hundred by the end of this month,' he says, flashing a toothless smile.

*

It is the twilight hour, just before darkness takes complete hold of our little world, when our neighbour Pu Thansiama walks in, a large heavy shawl wrapped to cover his missing arm. There were many stories about the arm, but my favourite by far was that he lost it because he was a child-eater and the people of his former village punished him by cutting his arm off. It was only after we were in the sixth grade that I began to let go of my stupid assumptions about the old man. He was, in fact, a friendly man, and was one of the few frequent visitors to our home.

'Have you heard the news? The MNF soldiers attacked the Aizawl Treasury,' he says with a heavy breath, as he takes big strides from the door towards Grandfather. 'They said they might declare independence tonight.' At the mention of the Aizawl Treasury, I immediately think of the squirrels in the banyan tree. Rini would be devastated if anything happens to the tree or the squirrels.

Zuala and I exchange glances and Grandfather beckons Pu Thansiama closer to him, probably afraid that we would overhear. But Grandfather is weak in the ears and he always speaks louder than needed, 'How unfortunate! Were there any shots fired?' His tone is a mixture of fear and excitement. 'Yes, yes, there was a firing. Not only that, they also robbed the treasury clean,' says Pu Thansiama as he pulls out a stool for himself near Grandfather and sets his heavy body on the poor thing. 'They said that the rebels have captured the police camps in Champhai and Lunglei too, though I'm not really sure if it's true. But I do know for sure that they've taken hold of the Aizawl Treasury and that they have ambushed the Assam Rifles headquarters.'

'Oh, what is the matter with our world now?' Grandfather sighs, emptying his pipe out of the window.

'Zuala, is your uncle home these days?' Grandfather inquires.

'He hasn't been home for more than two weeks now,' Zuala replies and then turns his head when he realizes what the question hinted at. 'Do you think he's there, at the firing?'

I immediately imagine Zuala's uncle carrying a rifle, moving about in the dark and picking his target. I know he will not be easily scared, but I do not want to imagine a rifle being pointed at him, though the picture comes close. I look at Zuala, wondering if he is having the same thoughts. I cannot tell.

'The rebels are fewer in number and have lower quality weapons than the soldiers. I fear for your uncle, Zuala. If things get worse, the rebels won't last more than a day or two. They'll be wiped clean,' says Grandfather slowly, like a soothsayer. The last sentence hangs in the air like a foul smell. Perhaps he thinks that it is important that Zuala know such things. Even Pu Thansiama seems a little shocked at what Grandfather said.

'Let's see if Laldenga will raise that white flag of independence tonight. How much exactly would be the price of freedom?' Pu Thansiama murmurs, as if talking to himself. Grandfather passes him the pipe and he taps it over the steel bowl, then returns it. Turning to Grandfather, he continues, 'I've always suspected that something of this sort would happen sooner or later. I think tonight will be the start of the real movement.'

Just then, Father barges in through the door. Upon seeing me and Zuala near the doorway, he clears his throat and straightens his tie, but I can tell that he is shaken. Father does not tremble unless he has a fever or has seen a ghost. And I have never seen him in either of these two situations.

'I was a bit worried about you,' I say as Father pulls out a stool and sits next to Pu Thansiama.

'I'm fine, son. We could hear the gunshots from Khatla Veng. It was quite loud,' says Father, realizing that it is no use hiding anything from us as he knows Pu Thansiama would not come over without news. 'Zuala, when did you come?'

'Right after dinner. I haven't even taken a proper bath. I think I should get going. It's safe to go out, isn't it?' Zuala asks.

'I think you shouldn't walk home alone,' Grandfather says, worried.

'Of course it's safe. Like Pu Thansiama said, our locality is far from the Treasury. There's nothing to be scared about,' Father says.

'Yes, yes. We're not kids anymore, Pu. Don't worry,' Zuala says with a toothless laugh.

'All right, you be careful, then,' says Father, fixing the level on the bag he had hung.

'Goodnight, then,' I say.

'Goodnight,' Zuala says before he disappears into the darkness.

I cannot understand what they are fighting for, the MNF rebels. I am perfectly fine with the way things are; I cannot imagine what more of freedom I need. Sometimes, I feel that people ask for too much. I mean I love collecting bullet casings, but I love being alive as well.

*

Looking back, that night seemed like an incident from ages ago and since then almost all the schools in Aizawl have been closed and the government offices not properly attended; it had become quite dangerous to freely roam on the streets, especially at night. The sound of gunfire had become a constant background noise day and night, but no one could get accustomed to it; we stayed indoors and life became more difficult than ever. The whole state of events was killing me and I was tired of being stuck at home with nothing else to do.

The impolite birds outside my window wake me up again. I walk into the kitchen and see that Grandfather is already at the table, holding the Bible. I barely ever see him reading anything else; I wonder if he ever comes across anything new in that book. He has his old shawl on and seems to be lost deep in thought. Maybe he is thinking about what might happen next, like a war tactician, both fearing and craving conflict. As he takes a sip of the steaming red tea, a mist forms on his glasses and he takes them off, momentarily looking at me with a big grin on his face. I reply with a lazy yawn.

'Oh,' he says, suddenly remembering something, 'Rini came when you were asleep. She was asking for you.'

'Did she tell you why?' I ask, trying to hide the excitement in my voice.

'No. She said she just came by to see you.'

'Can I go to her house to see her?'

'All right. But be careful. There are soldiers patrolling everywhere. Don't stay for too long. The two sides are constantly shooting at each other; we're just lucky that the shootings have not happened in our locality yet,' he says.

'That's between the MNF soldiers and the Indian Army. It's not like we're involved in this. I don't see any reason why we should be so scared. I'll be back soon,' I say and head towards the door. The very thought upsets me, that I have to be careful to see Rini. I can understand the need to be cautious when I go out with Zuala for cartridge hunting, but all Rini and I do is feed squirrels and talk and talk.

Rini lives right next to Mission Compound which is about a ten-minute walk from our house. As their house comes into sight, I see her waving her mother off to work. I notice her eyes lighting up the moment she sees me; I know mine did too.

'Grandfather told me you came over to see me.'

'Yes. I was wondering if you could come with me to Dawrpui,' she replies.

'Why? What for?' I ask in surprise.

'Mother had asked me to buy oil from Mr Pachhunga's place. She's afraid that the curfew might get worse. They're busy at the hospital, you know.'

In my head, I imagine all the bad things that can happen to us, like getting stuck in a crossfire or being captured as hostages by the Indian Army. But I quickly realize that this is the perfect chance to prove my worth to her.

'Sure. When shall we go?' I reply as casually as I can.

'Mother said we should go early before the curfew starts again.' It was already past eleven o'clock.

'Have you notice how just a few days ago words like 'curfew' were so new to us and now we're using them like we've known them since birth?' she says as we walk past Father's school.

'I've never thought of that,' I reply. It amazes me how her intelligence attracts me and makes me feel stupid at the same time.

'Things are changing so quickly. It's almost hard to believe, don't you think?'

'Well, I hate change,' I say grumpily.

'I want things to get better. So far, we're on the winning side,' she says with a smile on her face.

'Oh, I didn't know you're taking sides. As for me, I remain neutral and I hate all these curfews and whatnots.'

'How can you say that? There's not even the need to think which side we should take. Our people are fighting for us, for our independence. We just haven't realized the value of freedom because we've never been free before,' she says quite seriously. I want to side with her, but my head reminds me how much I hate the current situation.

'Well, I consider myself a free man. And I see no reason to fight for it.'

When we reach the Aizawl Treasury, which is on our way to school, there are a number of soldiers walking around. They look like they are waiting for something important. I stop to look at the big banyan tree and I breathe a sigh of relief on seeing that no damage has been done. But I realize that the cheerful chatterings of the squirrels are nowhere to be heard and the tree itself looks like it's warning us to go home. 'Where have they gone?' I whisper, almost talking to myself. Then, a line of army jeeps come running about, blaring announcements through a speaker. Rini and I stand still under the banyan tree, too afraid to move. I want to say something comforting to her, but my throat is strangely dry.

A loud crackling noise comes from the speaker and some loud taps, followed by a voice, 'This is an order given by District Commissioner T.S. Gill. No citizen will be allowed to stay outdoors from twelve noon. Everyone is ordered to stay at home.'

The voice coming from the speaker sounds like a pre-recorded one. The order is repeated again and again as the jeep moves around. There are two men with guns, standing in the back of the jeep. They look really frightening. I wonder if they had curfews in France and Germany during the World War. 'I think we should just go back. I don't feel safe staying out like this,' Rini says in a low voice, almost like a whisper. The few civilians in the streets are all walking in a hurry, heading towards their homes.

'Why do you have to whisper like that?' I ask, but what I really want to ask is if my presence beside her is making her feel safe even just a little bit. A light breeze blows her hair across her face and as she brushes her hair back and lightly gathers it behind her head. She asks me if I am scared at all.

'Not a bit,' I lie.

The streets are awfully quiet, except the sound of the jeep engines humming loudly. Few people are moving around and they all have this anxious look on their faces, including Rini. The announcement must have sent them home, I think. I am not scared enough to hurry home right away, but I am not at ease walking along the eerily quiet streets. Our house, with only three male occupants, is defined by silence and stillness most of the time. But not this kind of silence. Maybe there are silences that make your skin cold and the kind that makes you feel comfortably good. We walk through these streets every day on our way to school and now it feels different, like some unoccupied place and I feel like an unwanted presence.

There are policemen moving about here and there. As we pass the houses, I can see people peeping behind closed curtains, doors and windows shut, the sound of doors bolting from inside. A group of vegetable sellers walk past us in a hurry, their *empai* still stuffed with unsold vegetables and fruits. We immediately understand that the Thursday Bazaar has been closed for the day.

One policeman with a stern-looking face comes towards us and says, 'Which side of town are you from?'

'We're from Mission Veng, sir,' I reply, trying my best to sound as childlike as possible. I even give him a short smile, I think. Am I trying to woo a policeman to save my own life?

'Then why are you walking this way? Didn't you hear the announcement?' he asks, looking at us as if ready to beat us up with his long lathi.

'My mother sent us to collect some supplies from Dawrpui. We won't take long, sir,' Rini says with a straight face and a fake smile; fake because I knew her genuine one. I am trying my best to suppress my laughter, which is getting harder as she twists her lips and pretends like she is close to tears.

'Well, hurry up and go get your supplies, and get back home as soon as possible. The streets have to be cleared immediately,' the policeman says and walks away.

'How in the world did you do that?' I ask Rini who is laughing frantically as we walk on.

'I don't know,' she says amidst hysterical laughs. 'Stop laughing at me. My put-on voice saved us all right,' she says and gives me a slight push. I can see her set of clear white teeth as she laughs with her eyes half closed. I mimic her voice and she laughs some more. The world isn't such a bad place after all, I think to myself.

Then we suddenly become aware of the quietness along the almost empty streets and walk along in mutual silence. Perhaps, we are feeling guilty to be so happy in such a gloomy atmosphere. Like colours on a grey paper.

When we reach Dawrpui, we see Mr Hauva moving many of his stored merchandise out from the shop. A group of young men are loading the products on a long body jeep. He is busy counting the boxes and he doesn't seem to notice us walk by.

'I think he's planning to move away somewhere far,' Rini says to me in a whisper.

'I bet he has a trunkful of paper notes too,' I say admiringly. It is true. In Aizawl, Mr Hauva and Mr Pachhunga are well-known wealthy businessmen. They own concrete buildings, for God's sake! Mr Pachhunga's shop is at Chanmari, which is pretty far away so Rini's mother had told us to go to their house and ask if they had any stock.

We cross the road from Mr Hauva's shop and in a minute, we come face to face with a giant iron door. I ask Rini if she thinks the army bullets can shoot through it, but she hushes me and straightens her blouse and does a little touch-up on her hair after which she knocks on the door.

A woman with a calm oval-shaped face wearing a light green floral blouse opens the door. She is Mr Pachhunga's daughter-in-law.

'Oh, what a surprise! How can I help you?' she says in a motherly tone with a smile. I can tell from her voice that we gave her quite the scare. The rich are scared too, just like us. Maybe bullets can go through cement walls, I make a mental note to ask Zuala's uncle the next time I see him.

'Pi, my mother has sent us to see if you might have any oil to sell,' Rini asks.

She ushers us in briskly and says, 'Oh, child, I'm sorry, but we left all our merchandise at our shop.' She seems to feel genuinely bad to have let us down.

'But you know what, you can take home some of the stock we have here,' she rushes into a room and comes out with a medium-sized bottle of oil in her hand, a pack of sugar and salt.

'How much should we pay you?' Rini asks.

'Oh, that's not necessary, dear. At times like these, it's always good to be a blessing to others,' the woman says with a smile. If her lips had been slightly bigger, the smile would have looked pretty on her.

'Thank you so much,' Rini says and returns her smile, but a million times better.

When we get back on the streets, it is much quieter than before. I turn around to take another good look at the concrete building; it looks magnificent. It will be difficult for bullets to penetrate through the thick sturdy walls. The family living inside will surely survive even if a big attack takes place.

We head home in a hurry and I glance at Rini's flapping skirt every now and then. With the bottle of oil in her hand, she looks like someone from a story, probably a romance novel, maybe someone on a book cover.

'When are you ever going to tell her?' Zuala's voice echoes inside my head.

I uneasily drop her off and run back home as fast as my legs can carry me.

Night falls quickly and the moon is particularly bright. I watch it intently from my open window as thin sheets of clouds move slowly around it, as though teasing it. I think about Rini and imagine myself confessing my feelings to her. I begin to paint different scenes in my mind on how she would react—she gives me her signature smile, her eyes half closed and says that she had been waiting for me to tell her that, or one where she just looks at me as if I had said the forbidden word and tells me to never speak of it again. My favourite made-up scene is one where she blushes as I tell her how much I like her, her face glowing with that pinkish radiance as I slowly hold her delicate fingers in my shaky hands and, as I continue talking, she rests her head on my shoulder and after I finish my admission, she slowly lifts her face towards mine. Then, gathering all my courage, I kiss her lips. I do not want her to talk as I cannot imagine how she would respond in a situation like that.

While I am dreaming of Rini and her lips, I suddenly hear shots fired in the distance. I listen closer and realize that this isn't just a single gunshot but a continuous barrage. Father comes out from his room.

'Son, close the window and get back to bed quickly,' he says. It sounds like an order, so I make my move immediately.

'What's happening?' I ask.

'I think the soldiers have started to fire at each other again, but there's nothing to fear. I doubt that they will fight in this side of town. Just sleep with your pants on, all right? Just in case,' he says and retreats to his room without waiting for me to ask any further questions.

I know this one is different because the sound of the gunfire is closer than on any other night so far.

I cannot sleep at all. For a long moment, I sit on the edge of my bed and listen to the sound of gunfire going on and on as if it is just a normal late-night radio song trying to lull us to sleep. I force myself to get back to dreaming about Rini, but the only image that I can conjure up in my head is her small underlip curling in and closing again to say the word that she so often utters: freedom.

the
GEOMETRY
of SHAPES

sonaksha iyengar

I *taught* my body how to play

h
i
d
e

and

S E E k

hide
my body spills out of chairs
and tears the seams on XXXL dresses
jiggling, stomping, sprawling—
not words made for love letters
or coded into magic dreams,

never seek
they don't let me forget,
'your body—
is someone's shameful "before"
a metaphor for failure
a disclaimer for children
a poster child for loneliness.'

hide, and *never seek*, I am reminded,
nobody dreams of having a fat body
a fat body is no body
a fat body is nobody.

when the teacher asks us to present
a shape that resembles our bodies,
I mumble the rules of *hide* and *seek*,
hoping to fold myself into a dot
rectangle-rectangle-rectangle-triangle—

as the collective gaze crawls
from shape to person to shape
to me—I freeze
I see the sneers and smirks,
hide, and *never seek*
hide, and *never seek*

hide—
a shriek crawls from my belly
three parts anger, two parts tired

this is not a shape, this is my body
a museum to these memories,
a vessel to my pain,

this is not a shape
there are no points, no vertices, no lines
this body does not live in a maths class
no problem to be subtracted
no equation to be fixed

this is not a shape,
this is my body:
unfurling, expanding limits
sprawling across benches
stomping weighing scales
jiggling in bloom

a fat body is a body
a fat body is somebody
this fat body is *my* body.

Daddy's Girl[*]

Saina Nehwal

Μy sister Abu used to hate playing badminton against me when I was younger. 'She doesn't even know how to play,' she'd complain when my parents would ask her to play with me. I laugh about it now, while she feels a bit sheepish. Despite an age difference of seven years, we are very attached to each other.

When I started training, my entire family had to support my routine. Papa would come home from work, and it was always Abu who made him a cup of chai, as Mummy would take me to the stadium in the afternoons. Papa would then feed Macho, our dog, walk him and then head to the stadium to pick up Mummy and me. By the time we reached home, Abu would have dinner ready. I don't remember her complaining about the work she had to do, or the

---

[*] Excerpt from *Playing to Win* by Saina Nehwal (Penguin India, 2012)

attention that Mummy and Papa gave me. She was the quietly supportive one, who never seemed to resent me or the fact that I hogged all the limelight. She was a huge help for Mummy especially, silently taking over her chores. Through all this, she pursued her studies and graduated with a degree in pharmacy.

We lived very simply when I was growing up. There was neither time nor money to spend on eating out or going to the movies. All of us were focused on my training. Yet, no one ever seemed to mind the inconvenience of it all. If I remember correctly, Abu didn't even get a chance to come to the stadium to watch me play or travel with me those days, as she had to look after the house.

In 2007, Abu got married. It was a simple registered marriage; she made sure that my parents were not burdened with the expense of a lavish wedding. After her wedding, Abu moved to Delhi and we miss her immensely. Between her being in Delhi and my travels, there are few opportunities for the whole family to get together. But in 2009, when I returned to Hyderabad after my big wins, Abu was at the airport, waiting for me. I hadn't seen her since her wedding and it was so nice to be welcomed by her! She was holding her newborn baby Tawisha . . . I was now an aunt! Needless to say, it was celebration time at home. We now make it a point to meet once a year and when Abu is in Hyderabad, we have our girls' day out—visiting the spa and salon, watching movies, eating out . . . I look forward to her visits, as when she's at home, it's like a holiday we rarely have.

Mummy, like I said, is the ambitious one in the family. In fact, when I was born she had nicknamed me Steffi, after the legendary tennis player, Steffi Graf. In Hisar, I was known as Steffi to everyone, including my teachers and classmates, although Saina was my official name. It was only after we moved to Hyderabad that people started calling me Saina. But for Mummy, I am still Steffi.

Mummy is such a strong person and I have learnt a lot from her. For years, she played badminton, and also enrolled at the Hisar District Badminton Association. She played at the district level and in club tournaments, and some of her wins have been covered in the Hisar dailies. She continued to play even after Abu and I were born, and perhaps I inherited the game from her. After we moved to Hyderabad, Mummy stopped playing. Strangely, it coincided with me picking up the game. Mummy is tough, bold and resilient. If I have inherited anything from her, it's this toughness.

Having my family around has often made up for the lack of friends in my life. Mummy, Abu and I have always been close. Until Abu got married, Sundays were our special holidays. With Mummy's exceptional cooking skills, our Sunday lunches were always the highlight of the day.

Attached as I am to both Abu and Mummy, I am a self-confessed daddy's girl! In the rural north, there is a saying 'Pitro mukhi sada sukhi', which roughly translates to 'A girl with her father's face is always happy'. I think I take after my father. For years, Papa has always been by my side, seeing me through my training. I've never heard him complain about the physical stress or the financial crunch. But for his quiet and relentless support, I would not have been able to reach this far.

For a long time, I had no idea that my racquets were so expensive. I used to be very careless with them, losing them easily. It was when journalists asked me how I managed without sponsors that I went up to Papa and asked him in turn. I was shocked to hear that he had been borrowing from his provident fund savings to pay for my training and my kit! From the time I started playing, in 1999, until 2004 when I got my first sponsor, Papa paid the bills. The racquets would cost around Rs 14,000 and I would need at least two at any given point. A barrel of shuttles cost a thousand rupees and I would use up some two barrels a day! Apart from the equipment, there were my shoes, clothes, tickets to pay for when we travelled to tournaments—not just for me but also Mummy, who would accompany me—our hotel bills and other incidentals. I would notch up a bill of Rs 50–60,000 a month and Papa would quietly keep paying up without letting on how difficult it was. And for a long time, there was no way of knowing that I would be successful at the game. Thankfully, I started winning at tournaments and his sacrifice was not for nothing.

Where Mummy believes in hard work as the answer to getting what you want from life, Papa is all for finding one's way around life. In badminton, Mummy advocates learning every tactic whereas Papa says, 'Find out what works for you and learn that well.' Mummy focuses on the result and Papa's philosophy is to work hard and never mind the results. Although both have influenced me, over time, I find myself more inclined towards Papa's way of thinking. I am less hard on myself these days and do only what I need to do for a good game.

For a long time, Mummy would travel with me, sit in the front row and guide me through the match. She has a knack for saying the right things at the right time and I find her presence very helpful. Papa used to find it hard to watch me play. Even watching me on TV would make him nervous and for a long time, whenever my match was on, he would head out for a walk and stay out until I called. He was always the first one I would call, whether I won or lost. In 2010, when I was headed for the All England Championships, I thought it would be nice to have him come along for a change. It still wasn't easy for him to watch me play. At first, he would stand outside the court, waiting for some of my teammates to tell him what was happening. But now, when I am on court, I see him in the audience. I can hear him cheering and guiding me, and that makes me smile.

After that trip, Papa started accompanying me on several tournaments. And it has been a huge support for me to have him around. I am not the friendliest nor the most social person and having my dad with me gives me all the support I need. Earlier, he would be so frustrated seeing my packed suitcases lying around. I used to insist that it was just easier to have them packed and ready to go. And now I see his suitcase lying in wait next to mine! Papa has also shown me how to deal with being a celebrity. His advice was simple—be humble. When journalists come home to interview me, he is always polite to them; when the phone rings, he answers politely and doesn't brush anyone off. Truth be told, sometimes I think he is more popular with journalists than I am. I don't enjoy interviews all that much and try to keep them brief. Sometimes, a journalist will call up Papa and ask him for a sound bite, instead of me. And I am quite happy to let him do the talking. Papa also keeps track of all the media coverage. He keeps the paper clippings and loves to read them again and again. And he'll remind me of how far I have come. I also have a manager now, Manjula, and Papa coordinates my schedule with her. But for him, I'd have no idea what's happening outside of my game. He spends hours making sure my finances are in order, my schedule is not too messy and my bills are paid.

As you can see, I owe a great deal to Papa. On 1 July 2010, I was invited to the head office of the Indian Council of Agricultural Research (ICAR) where Papa works. I had been made the brand ambassador of ICAR and Papa was so proud. His colleagues have been extremely supportive of him, and me. But for that, it would have been difficult for him to take time out to be with me. In fact, the first time I ever signed an autograph was for Papa's colleagues. I was ten years old and had won the Under-10 district-level tournament. When I went to Papa's office, his colleagues said they had read about me in the paper and asked for my autograph. I remember looking at Papa, who nodded, and I signed my name for them. And now, after all these years, I was very happy to be able to give back something, and that I could do this for my papa.

For Papa, I am still his baby. He calls me Shiny, Tapi, Baccha . . . Sometimes he calls me Abu and I have to remind him that I am Saina, not Abu.

My take on life and other stuff:

\# Having dreams: A positive sign of progress and of a creative mind

\# Following your dreams: A must to turn them into reality

\# Hard work and discipline: Integral to progress

\# Education: As important as sports

\# Money: Unfortunately, in India, people judge you by it

\# Fame and success: Compatible with a person who believes in his or her own strength

\# Winning and losing: The two realities in sports

\# Staying grounded: Will bring prosperity and popularity among well-wishers

\# Patriotism: Our moral duty is to respect the people and the country to which we belong

\# Coaches: No two ways about it, we must respect our gurus as they are the ones who open the path to our success

\# Parents: Should be number one in our lives

\# Responsibilities: Deal with them! Working hard, staying focused and disciplined, believing in the Creator, whatever name one calls him by, will help shoulder them.

An Accidental Ambition

Japleen Pasricha

I was an average student in school, the most average person you'd know. I had accepted that in my formative years. I was neither that girl who scored the first rank nor was I a popular girl. I didn't have many friends either. I never had high ambitions or even expansive dreams. The thought of becoming a doctor, engineer or lawyer never occurred to me because these professions were way out of my league, or so I thought! I didn't need someone to protect my ego or say otherwise. I was absolutely okay with being this person. I want to believe that my parents had similar thoughts and were content that I passed my exams with marks that were just above average every single time.

We were in a well-lit room in my junior school in R.K. Puram in New Delhi. My teacher was going from one white-shirt-wearing pupil to another, asking them what they wanted to be when they grew up while

I sat in the corner of the classroom dreading my turn. 'Ma'am, I want to become an astronaut!' someone said. A doctor, engineer, architect, lawyer, teacher, nurse and scientist followed.

The teacher was closing in and I had absolutely no idea what to say. I frantically looked here and there, trying to come up with something smart, but our brain always works in mysterious ways and never helps us when we need it the most, right? Stupid brain! Finally, when the teacher turned to me and said, 'Japleen, what do you want to become?' 'Umm . . . teacher, ma'am,' I fumbled, cursing myself in my mind.

'Wow, so original, Japleen!'

I had hated this question ever since. Every time teachers, parents, relatives and even friends asked me this question, I found myself getting more annoyed. Why do we have to become something or someone? I didn't have time for this nonsense. *Could I first focus on my midterm exams, please,* I wanted to yell back. While everyone around me wanted to be something, anything, I was happy being average.

I still think of that day sometimes. Today, I'm a feminist activist and a successful media entrepreneur. I founded and lead Feminism in India—an award-winning digital feminist media platform with an all-women's team to learn, educate and develop a feminist sensibility among the youth. Sounds crazy, right? As young students, we are pressured into deciding what we want to do at fifteen or sixteen years of age. I didn't find my calling until I was twenty-five and three degrees down! And who's to say that I can't still change my career? But that's for another time. Let me tell you the story of how an average girl who thought she loved teaching created India's most popular feminist website and 'taught' feminism to many, many girls and women.

Not too long after the dreaded Q&A round with our teacher, I was given a choice of choosing between German or Sanskrit as a third language. My elder sister had picked German when offered the same choice, so I just went with the road (only previously) taken. And what use is Sanskrit anyway!

I was very excited for my first German class and even learnt some words like *mutter, vater, bruder, schwester* (mother, father, brother and sister) beforehand, to impress my teacher and classmates (courtesy of my sister's old notebooks). As it turned out, I was surprisingly good at German! Good enough to make my parents surprise me with an iPod when I got 91 marks in German in my 10th grade exams. This was 2005 by the way, so an iPod for a middle-class family was pretty huge!

I was also happy, naturally! Since my 'marks' told me that I was good at German and I enjoyed the language, I decided there and then that this is what

I'd do when I grew up—learn German academically. I was fifteen then, but I had a very clear idea of my 'German' ambition.

The next few years were a blur of being a not-so-average-hey-I-am-actually-good-at-this German student. I became the class topper and the teacher's pet during my three years of studying German at the University of Delhi. Not only did I top all three years of my BA, I received two scholarships to study in Germany, spent practically most of my third year in Berlin (I know!) and received a gold medal from the chancellor of the university. I was literally on top of the world. I was headed towards my goal of being a German language professor.

While most of my peers went for corporate jobs with handsome salaries, I decided to continue further with German. I wanted to study pedagogy and teach German. It was a match made in heaven, or so I believed.

The year was 2012 and I had just finished my MA and enrolled in MPhil at the Jawaharlal Nehru University in New Delhi. But something just wasn't right. Mind you, I loved teaching, I still do, but for the first time in years, I was back to feeling unsure about what I was doing. You see, this was just about the time when we learnt about the 2012 Delhi gang rape and murder case. As a young girl in her early twenties living in Delhi, I was frustrated beyond limits. Till then I had accepted how a young girl is treated in India. Of course, I had to be back by 7 or 8 p.m. And it was okay that I had never celebrated New Year's Eve out with my friends because I was never allowed. Conversations in my extended family about how my parents were expecting a boy when I was born or how they should have tried for another child because our family is 'incomplete' infuriated me. I would constantly argue with my relatives till I broke down and cried my heart out.

Curfews, casual sexism, stalking, street and sexual harassment, differential treatment—these were just some of the things that I had normalized. I felt so wronged and violated! We as individuals still do. On top of that, there would be everyday cases of rape, discrimination and violence against women in the news. These incidents and dialogues began to fill my head. I was distressed and felt I had to do something about it. We all did. It's all so many women around the country talked about.

One wintery day in March, huddled in my bed, I was reading the book *Feminism in India*. On a whim, I opened Facebook and created a page called Feminism in India (FII). Mind you, this was 2013 and Instagram and Snapchat were not the rage yet. Perhaps it was out of boredom or frustration fuelled by everyday sexism, memories of being stalked on my way home and being harassed in the streets, at times by men I knew. Or perhaps it was because a few years previously, on my way to college, I had been molested on the Delhi Metro. A memory I had repressed and 'moved on' from. This was before Delhi Metro had a women's compartment. A man was rubbing his private parts against my body in a very busy and crowded metro. The moment I saw it, I froze and quickly got out of the compartment. I didn't say anything to anyone and went home quietly. The incident completely shattered me and I continued to blame myself for keeping quiet, for not raising an alarm, for going into a shock and not doing anything.

In mid-2013, I was in Germany, as a part of some research work I had to undertake for my MPhil. I began blogging mostly about personal experiences. I wrote about the pressure of arranged marriages that young women have to face in India, about rape culture and how politicians and law enforcement tend to blame the victim rather than the perpetrator, about menstrual taboos and stigma, about safety for women in Germany as compared to India. Even though I was living in Germany, my heart was in India. I would constantly think about what was happening back home. Many people, including my parents, would tell me that I should just 'settle down' in Germany, that it was a better place to live in, and safer for women. I could, but I didn't want to. I guess, I'm one of those emotional fools who didn't just want to make a better world for herself, but for many more women around her.

I used the Facebook page and the blog to vent and interact with like-minded feminist bloggers. It became a safe space where I would also share feminist content from around the internet. Because I was still writing my MPhil thesis, I wasn't very sure what I wanted to do with this page, but with each passing day my conviction that this is my calling grew stronger.

A year later, I woke up at 2 a.m. with an idea! I had seen photo campaigns called 'I Need Feminism Because . . .' on a few feminist groups and I was instantly inspired. 'I Need Feminism . . .' (INF) was a public awareness campaign where men and women are asked why and how feminism is important to them. The campaign was directly inspired from a similar campaign held at Oxford University and Cambridge University, which later became a rage in many campuses across the globe. The campaign was also organized in Pakistan by the Lahore University of Management Sciences (LUMS). I thought, *why not India!* I called my friend Gayatri right away. We were going to create India's first INF campaign.

The idea quickly turned into an event with the help of Gayatri, who was then a student at Indira

Gandhi Institute of Technology (IGIT, a women-only technology institute in Delhi) and her friends. We also reached out to professors and students in the gender studies department and took permission to extend the campaign to Ambedkar University Delhi (AUD). We decided on a date, created a Facebook event page, invited students and friends we knew.

On 15 April 2014, Gayatri and I, along with lots of enthusiastic volunteers, were ready to kick-start the INF campaign at IGIT and AUD. To break the ice, we started by asking people what they understood by the term 'feminism'.

Soon people started warming up to the idea and powerful slogans began to emerge from these conversations that we ran around documenting.

I need feminism . . .
because I want to go out into the streets, carefree.
because gender roles shouldn't dictate my life, the
        way I carry myself, what I wear.
because I don't need to be told whom to love.
because I have a story to tell.
to assert my own individuality.
because I want my daughter to live in a better
        world than I did.
because equality should be a fundamental right.
because I want unqualified freedom.

By the end of the day, we had exceeded our initial target of photographing 100 thoughts on 'I Need Feminism Because . . .' The campaign was featured on multiple news and media platforms. India's first-ever 'I Need Feminism' campaign, organized and executed by young students keen to bring about a change in popular mindset as well as action, was a huge success. This was before BuzzFeed and Bollywood celebrities did it, they mostly took inspiration from our campaign but never credited us, by the way!

The overwhelming response at the event inspired me to organize more events—offline and online. I couldn't stop now. It was at this point that the fog I had been in started to lift. This was the first time I indulged in 'activism' and although shy initially, I was in the groove by the third or fourth campaign. My love affair with German was over. My parents were very unsure of this and asked me to find a 'balance' where I could do both. Most people asked the same question again and again, 'You're doing so well in this subject, why do you want to change it?'

On the surface, it looked like I had everything I wanted and things were fine and they were. But sometimes you don't have a clear answer as to why you want to do something different, even though it may look illogical to others. So many aunties and uncles we know laud conventional career choices and defying those paths is viewed with a lot of suspicion. It wasn't easy to let go and start from scratch, but the heart wants what it wants. Stupid heart! I had to give my calling a chance, even if I failed. Some people felt like I did not know what I was doing by embracing gender activism—changing goals after a certain point is seen as a sign of being lost. Some would say I was being incredibly stupid and I'd agree with them. But if you ask me, I felt a new-found confidence and passion for something I believed in and loved doing.

At twenty-five years of age, I left behind twelve years of a chosen career and switched from German to *drum roll* Gender. I guess I finally knew what I wanted to become. I know it was pretty late but the problem is not the question, but society's expectations of young people. We are not given that space to explore, make mistakes, change our decisions and try out new things. I'm so happy that I did get that opportunity and that my family stood by me. They understood that I needed to do something that I strongly believed in.

Honestly, I had no plan, but I had conviction. I had absolutely no academic or work experience in gender, women's rights or feminism and struggled with finding jobs in the development sector. Even though I had three academic degrees and was overqualified for most of the jobs out there, everything I had done so far was irrelevant to what I wanted to do.

I wrote to NGOs that worked for women's rights and on gender in New Delhi for volunteer work, internships or jobs. I didn't hear from anyone. I joined feminist groups on Facebook so that I could network with like-minded people and attend events and seminars on gender and feminism. Often, the stories we read and hear about are success stories of people who made it and make it look easy. But nobody talks about unanswered emails and rejections because I got rejected everywhere. My motivation, passion, grit and determination weren't as important as my degrees and grades.

I finally found a job after about seven months of searching, at a Delhi-based non-profit organization working to end violence against women. With the job search out of the way, I turned my attention to my page (FII) and what I wanted to do with it.

With FII, I began my own journey of being a feminist. I decided that I had to create a space for Indian feminism, voiced by Indian feminists. We needed a space where one could read easy-to-understand, accessible, popular Indian feminist content on the internet written by Indian women for Indian women, a space where one could connect with like-minded people and a space where one could find resources related to women's issues and gender, a space without judgement, a space to find comfort through uncomfortable conversations. We needed feminism to step away from the realm of academics and theory and into our everyday conversations.

Slowly, people began to engage with the page and I built up a nascent digital feminist community. So when I put out my plans of creating a website, I immediately began receiving offers to contribute to the website.

FII started with publishing one or two crowdsourced articles a week. The goal was to include the voices of more women and people from communities that are otherwise forgotten and marginalized. To share their stories and their histories and amplify these usually unheard stories using digital storytelling techniques, pop culture references, photo stories, videos and whatever other media was emerging online.

I was juggling my job at the non-profit organization while nurturing my passion for FII. Every day after work, I would sit with my laptop and think of new ways to engage those around me with feminism.

So, in late 2014, having decided that I had hidden from my own experiences on the Delhi Metro for too long, I conceptualized a campaign where young women would write about their stories of sexual harassment. I wanted to tell girls and women that sexual harassment had absolutely nothing to do with their clothes, behaviour, where they were, what they were doing or the many other things that they were often blamed for. Sexual harassment is never the victim's fault and someone had to say it out loud.

I wrote my own story, reliving those moments for days, and invited other women to take part in this cathartic exercise. Women I didn't know began reaching out to me to share their stories of sexual harassment. I remember a young woman who messaged me at the onset of the campaign and said that although she loved what the campaign was doing, she wasn't able to find enough courage to write her own story. I assured her that it's completely okay if she wasn't not ready. However, a few days later, she wrote back saying that after reading so many stories from other women, she felt comfortable sending in her story.

This, right there, was the success I needed— that I and this campaign were able to give a young woman courage and assurance to speak about her own experiences. It means that when one woman stands up for herself, she stands up for everyone! Our silence is seen and there will always be a safe space to talk about our experiences and find comfort. That we're not alone.

We were able to collate and publish sixteen stories and a year later, it won the prestigious Laadli Media Award for gender sensitivity!

There was no looking back from then. After working at two different non-profit organizations for two years, I was ready to fly solo. I quit my full-time job in 2016 and focused on FII full-time. I had never really thought about starting my own organization and becoming an entrepreneur, but sometimes life just takes its own road and you have to follow it to find your path.

Though an entrepreneur's journey may look glamorous and ambitious on the outside and I know, as I read this piece, it all sounds exciting, but it's a very lonely and difficult journey. I spent that year researching business plans, learning how to run an organization, how to raise funds and writing grant applications. I had absolutely no idea how to do any of this. I didn't have a co-founder, a management degree or any experience.

I would study social media trends and analytics, read news articles every day to understand how one writes and edits a news piece or opinion- and analysis-based articles, write grant applications and annual reports. I worked on developing and customizing our website. Everything that I do today, I have learnt on the job.

After many failed grant applications, I cracked our first round of funding and started the process of registering the organization, looking for a co-working space, hiring and the usuals of running any entity. I hired my first employee in 2017 and we used to work out of a small cabin just enough for 2–3 people in a co-working space.

Luckily, I did find support in my parents and friends, who despite disagreeing or not understanding why I would leave a flourishing academic career to get into a media start-up, still supported me.

From one, we became two to three to five and today we're an all-women's team of eleven. The media industry in India is mostly dominated by men. In such a context, having an all-women's team leading a feminist media publication is not only empowering for me but also for so many young women out there who don't have enough role models to look up to.

As an entrepreneur working on feminism, I have been told many times to 'stick to women's issues only and not talk about larger socio-economic issues in the country'. This statement comes from the assumption that women have nothing to do with the business and politics of running a country but can only talk about 'conventional' issues related to women. How wrong are those people! Everything is a woman's issue: from domestic chores to the country's budget, from menstrual taboos to political representation, from sexual harassment to financial investment. Gender is everywhere and as feminists we explain day in and day out that it is necessary to analyse everything from the lens of people pushed into the margins.

For me, feminism is simply social justice. It views the world from the lens of those who have been pushed to the margins and fights for their rights and justice. I understand feminism not just to be about the empowerment of women, but a dissolution of all oppressive social structures—patriarchy, casteism, queer and transphobia, ableism and many more, all included. Feminism is a process, and it takes a lot of unlearning and relearning. I believe that I am still learning and will do so for the rest of my life.

I'm so proud of the work I have done till now and the organization and the team I have built. I once attended a workshop called 'I'm Remarkable'—some might consider it rather narcissistic—where I learnt that achievements are based on facts and there is nothing wrong in speaking out about your achievements and being proud of them.

Young girls and women are specifically hardwired into not showing off their work, not speaking out about their accomplishments and playing down their ambitions. I internalized the same and I'm trying to change that not just for myself but for my team members, the feminist community I work in and any young woman and girl who is reading this and has a brilliant idea or has high ambitions. If you are proud of what you've done, say it out loud.

If I could give my younger self one piece of advice or even just talk to her from where I stand, I'd say, 'Never let anyone tell you that your marks in school, degrees in university or your past experiences will define your ambition. Never think of yourself as just average and never ever believe people who tell you it's too late to follow your dreams. If I know you, you are rolling your eyes at me for this cliché, but this is true. You didn't become a teacher in the conventional sense of the word, and I have to admit, you will miss being in the classroom with a bunch of excited students in front of you and your whiteboard behind. But, I do think, you're still teaching. You're ensuring that young people today understand feminism, read about our country's rich history of the women's movement and learn how to make this world a bit more just for themselves and for others.'

You Have 1 Follower

Jane De Suza

'Invisible.'

'Invisible what?' The principal leans forward. Her office is huge, and the polished desk between us gleams so much I can see myself in it. There is a wall of trophies behind her, but I like staring out of the big window instead.

'Divya? Care to expand on that?'

'No.'

'It's been a long day at school, and I'm sure you want to go home. But we do need to talk about it, Divya. It's 4 p.m. now, and this shouldn't take more than half an hour. So, what is "invisible"?'

I stare out. The sky is a harsh, glaring afternoon orange.

'Your life could be in danger. I'd have no choice but to report it to the police. But first, just you and me. Should we start with the facts? You have a good academic record, good health, good friends and—'

'No.'

'No friends? Come on, Divya, what about Satish and—'

'He's shorter than me.'

'And that disqualifies him? I see.'

She's annoying. This woman who runs the school and thinks that, by extension, she runs my life. She thinks she knows her students. She doesn't. Not even a bit. I decide to tell her that.

'You don't. None of you people see anything. I'm SIXTEEN! That's the age when everyone else is high on life, on "likes", on being the focus of the picture. Me? I'm not even in the picture. You don't know what it's like. Kannikka, ya? You know her. Everyone knows her, wants to be with her, sees her . . . me, no one sees me. You don't believe me? So the other day at Slop!—the ice cream place? We are there and I feel someone's eyes on me. Hot. You know you can feel it. I turn and Pranav's staring at me. The 12th grader Pranav, you know, who did that speech on World Environment Day? So, he's staring. And I sort of smile. He smiles back. Five minutes later, he's still staring. He nods sideways and so I make up some excuse like I gotta go to the loo, and I go to where he is standing by the counter, and he goes Hi, could you help me? Please. Give me Kannikka's number. Please. Please.'

'Divya, are you saying Pranav is the one who is threatening you now?'

'No! I don't know. I'm scared, that's all.'

'I know, Divya. I'm here to help.'

'So help me answer this. Why me? Why is this perv targeting me? No one targets me, no one even notices me. I'm supposed to be invisible. Why not Kannikka or one of those cute girls?'

'You don't think you're cute?' She tilts her head at me. 'Why not? You can be frank with me, you know? I've always told my students that.'

She wants frank? She'll get frank.

'Stop patronizing me, please, Shenaz Miss. I'm brainy. But cute? Just ask me your questions and I'll answer. Frankly. And I can go home earlier then.'

'What would you like me to ask you, Divya?'

'Ok, I'll make this quicker myself. When did I first get targeted? Should we start there?'

'If you like . . .'

'I would like to go home, so yes. The first time. In the school bus on the way home. We all get into the bus, and this 6th grader kid picks up something from the floor of the school bus and gives it to me. It's a card with a heart cut out on the front. And inside, it says: DIVYA, YOU STOLE MY HEART. In bright green ink, in capitals. I stare at the kid who stares back at me. And then, the others are like Let me see, let me see, and everyone's passing the card around and at first, they're laughing. Like Divya's got a follower, oooh! And all that—then it gets serious, the chatter. The girls are all like You know who it is? And I stare at them, like, no, I don't have a clue. I was sure it was some stupid prank. And by the time I get off the bus, I see it in their eyes. Curiosity. Envy.'

I stop to drink coffee. Ha! One of the plus points of going to the Princi's office. You get offered coffee from the staff coffee machine. Very adult! It's like if you've got issues, you're suddenly very adult. The principal says, 'And how did this make you feel?'

I choke. 'You're serious? How would you feel if some perv threatens you, follows you, stalks you, attacks you?'

The principal, she just looks at me. I want to act the brat. To provoke her into reacting. But she's not.

I lean in. 'I'm sure someone's making a fool of me. I feel targeted. I don't like being a target. It's like this huge, horrible prank. I like being invisible. And then you know what happened two days later . . . We're all sitting in class, first period, and the gateman—the security at the main gate—he knocks on the classroom door. There's an urgent message for Divya S., class 10 B, from her father. It was stuck on the gate. Principal Madam says to give it to her at once, he says. That's you, so you know this. My heart's thudding already.

It's a sealed envelope and the physics teacher stops the class till I tear it open. All okay, Divya? she's asking. And I'm holding the note, and Neeti, next to me, reads it aloud. Miss, it's from her father, saying to come to the main gate now—he wants to meet her. And I look at the green all caps, and say slowly, No, Miss. My father is not in town, he's away on work. It must be some prank. What I don't say aloud but I know—and the girls all know is—it's HIM!'

'Did you go to the gate, Divya?' the principal asks.

'No. The physics teacher told the gateman to call her on her mobile if he saw my father come to the gate. She took the note away too. And I'm assuming she gave it to you? And that's why I'm here? Because it's a serious threat to a student of this school.'

'Divya, this IS serious. What did your parents say?'

'You're kidding, Miss? You think I'd tell them? They'd go mental.'

'Did you try telling them?'

'No. I can't. I can't disturb them with silly stuff like this. They've got way too much on their minds already. Mom's always on calls—overseas calls—so like all hours of the day. And Dad's away on work—for days together, often.'

'Divya, they have to know if you're in danger.'

'No. They know enough. If you tell them any more, I will stop talking to you. I swear.'

I push back my chair.

'Wait! Divya, wait. What you tell me is confidential. I won't share it with anyone, unless I deem you to be in serious danger. Do you understand? If someone is stalking you, that connotes the possibility of physical danger.'

I stand up. 'I'm not talking anymore.'

The principal keeps sitting. 'You're free to leave. But I am here to help you. I want you to know that.'

'Don't you have a family to go home to?' I glance pointedly at the clock on the wall, and nod at the photo frame on her desk. 'We all saw your two cute kids at the flag hoisting on Republic Day. Why are you sitting here with me? Oh ya—it's because it's your job. So if I stay talking till midnight, you've got to sit here too?' I smile. To show her it's a joke.

Nothing. No reaction.

I go to the door. 'Bye! Go home, Shenaz Miss, you're free to leave.'

She still doesn't say anything. Super irritating! I slam the door on the way out.

The school is deserted after class hours. I see the old cleaner turning off the lights in the classrooms, going from room to room, locking the doors behind him. I stand in a corner and stare at the door of the Princi's office. It doesn't open.

Finally, I go back and open it myself. Push it. Pop my head in. She's still sitting there. I go back in and sit on the chair again. 'Had to go to the loo. Bet you thought I was leaving, ya?' I smile like I've scammed her. She smiles. A little.

'Do you want me to accompany you home today? Are you afraid of this stalker?'

'Wow, the principal dropping me home? Very wow! And of course I'm scared of him. I keep looking around. Wouldn't you? He's a lunatic. Deranged. Dangerous.'

She nods. 'I would be afraid, yes.'

'And what would you have done?'

'I think it could be a case for the police.'

I take another sip from that cup of coffee. So adult. I imagine the teachers drinking from cups like this in the staffroom and talking about students. Talking about ME. *That Divya*, they will be saying, *she's* . . .

'So!' I look at the principal. 'So where were we?'

'He'd sent you a sealed envelope and was waiting outside the school gate to meet you.'

'Ya. So now the girls all surround me. Wherever I go, there's this gang. They're protecting me but also a little curious, you know? Like who's this dude? Another student? Teacher? Parent? Ugh! Because these two notes have been connected to school, ya? So they're trying to guess who it could be, who could have crept into the school bus before anyone else saw them. Was it the cleaner? Remember that case recently when the—'

The principal looks up because I've stopped suddenly. I've got this lump in my throat out of nowhere. I reach for my water bottle, uncap it and gulp.

'Is it the cleaner, Divya? Did anything happen? Did he say anything to you at any other point of time? Did you notice anything?'

'No! He's a sweet old man, and the other ones are women. They're all nice. I screamed at the girls and they shut up. It's my life they're fooling around with. This guy's scary! I could be kidnapped. I have to keep looking over my shoulder nowadays. What if—you know—what if?'

'And he's someone at school, you think?'

'I didn't say that. The girls did.'

'But you say the notes are only at school?'

'No. They started there.'

'And then?'

'Shenaz Miss! He followed me home. He knows where I live. He even followed me to Slop! So he knows we go there after school sometimes.'

She frowns. I must admit she does react then. She looks concerned when she asks, 'Did you see him?'

'I don't know. Maybe. We kept looking out for someone suspicious. But if you're looking out like that—every guy looks suspicious. That Pranav is always staring . . .'

'Again, could it be Pranav? You won't be in any trouble for naming anyone . . .'

'No! He's crushing on Kannikka. And he's too stupid to be stalking anyone—they'd find him at once.'

'How did you know he was at the ice cream place, Divya?'

'The guy at the counter called out loud, over the music, like Who's DIVYAS? And the girls looked at me. It's Divya, I said. Divya S. That's my initial. Why? And he's like, You've left your box on the counter. And I've not left anything, ya? So I go there, scared, and Neeti goes with me, and the other girls too—like holding my arm and all. And there's this box there, with my name on it. I look at them, frightened. And their eyes are wide. And they say Open it. And I say, No, it's time we report this now. And they're like, Just see what's inside.'

'Yes, it would have been wiser to report it.'

'But there were chocolates, Shenaz Miss. And that's like—that's not a crime—is it? Half a dozen chocolates, you know that kind where each one is in a little paper cup? So we all go Yay! And all that and they dive in. And we're laughing and struggling to grab a chocolate. And Kannikka says, Dude, your stalker may be a creep, but he has great taste! And with the chocolate in my mouth, like making this big lump in one cheek, I spot a note, at the bottom of the box. When it's empty, you can see the note. And I point at it, shivering.'

'Did anyone see the person who left the box?'

'Someone may have. But it's so crowded. You've got to fight for a bench. Or even fight to get to the counter. Anyway. There's this note. It says: I FEEL THIS EMPTY WITHOUT YOU. YOU DON'T CARE ABOUT ME!'

I pause and look at her. She nods, 'It is escalating, Divya. He's showing signs of getting desperate.'

'Exactly! Neeti asks the counter guy if he saw anyone leave the box, and he says guys are always leaving things—phones and files. No big deal. They'll come back and get it later. We ask about CCTV and he laughs and says it's long since bust, sorry.'

Then I continue, 'We fall silent. I feel like there's something creeping over me, inch by inch, creepy-crawling across my skin. I tell the girls that. I say, "It's gone too far." We look around. They say Maybe it's that guy, or maybe it's that one.'

'Who says?'

'The other girls. We're all guessing now. There's this guy with a beanie.'

'A what? Some kind of coffee?'

'That cap thing. Oh, let me draw it for you.' I scribble and she nods.

'So he's looking at us, ya? He's all alone and he's staring at us. And then Neeti suddenly goes up to him, shouting, I'll show the—well, I won't use that word with you, ok? But I'm like, Neeti, stop, what are you doing? But you know what Neeti's like, ya?'

'I don't really, I'm sorry . . . What's Neeti like?'

'Really? I thought you knew all your students well. Ha! She's the long jump champ. And she's tall and anyway, so she goes up to him. And . . .' I laugh.

The principal doesn't laugh.

I shrug, 'Ya, so Neeti comes back a bit later and we're all like, What happened? Is he the perv? And she says, No, he's cute actually. And we groan. And she says she confronted him and asked him why he was staring and he said it was because we were all screaming and gasping and didn't we realize the whole crowd in there was staring at us?' I laugh again. That moment cracks me up.

The principal doesn't laugh. I'm getting fed up now. Time to end this.

'Ya. So! Not him.'

She looks at some notes on her desk. 'One of your friends mentioned the stalker dashing out of there, and your seeing him?'

'Oh, that! This random guy. He just dashed out of Slop! You know? Just ran.'

'Did you catch a glimpse of him? What he looked like?'

'Neeti and Kannikka ran after him, but they couldn't keep up. He got on to a bike and sped off.'

'What did he look like, Divya, did they say?'

'Normal. Average height. Average build. Ya. Average. Not him.'

'How do you know that?'

'Because he was some delivery app guy with that food box on his bike, so had to rush with the order.'

'But he could have been your stalker?'

'No! He wasn't even stalking. He just rushed off. Haha!' I try a dry laugh. Not tough. My throat's parched.

'Look, it was NOT him, I'd know him if I saw him.'

'How?'

'A girl knows these things.' I sip the coffee. Adultlike, you know.

'Divya, I have to ask. What do you know about him? Anything that you're holding back? You can tell me.'

'Shenaz Miss. I've got to go home. My folks will be worried now.'

'Don't worry, we've informed them.'

'What? What did you tell them? I told you not to alarm them.'

'It's under control, Divya, I spoke to them myself. It's quite ok. You can leave when you want to. If you think they're worrying about you, you could call them now?'

'No!' I look out the window. 'They won't worry. You're right.'

I stare out at the sky. My eyes are watering. I can't say anything. I don't. There's this long silence. She doesn't talk. I don't talk.

Finally, she breaks it. 'Divya,' she says gently, 'this is dangerous. Your stalker could be anyone. A delivery guy, a driver, a classmate. Don't rule anyone out.'

I say nothing.

'Do you suspect someone else? Someone you know well?'

I yawn, stretch my arms out and look at the clock. 'Shenaz Miss, this is going round in circles. You want me to name someone so we can wrap this all up, ya?'

'Do you want to give me a name? No one will get into trouble, I promise, if you tell me.'

'I want to end this all.'

'Ok. What do you want to do?'

'To finish talking to you—and then it's over. Your job. And you don't ask me anything anymore. I'll tell you about the last note.'

'When did you get that?' She looks down at the paper on her desk.

'Last weekend. He followed me home. And my mom found his note this time. It was under the windscreen wiper on her car. It said in that same horrible green ink: STOP IGNORING ME! YOU'RE HEARTLESS!! YOU DON'T CARE!!!'

The principal waits when I stop, chewing my lip.

'That's it. Last note.'

'And this was the one that caused all the trouble, right, Divya?'

I hate myself, but I'm full-on crying now.

'Yes. When I told Kannikka, she told everyone else. And on Monday morning, the guys surrounded Satish and began to push him around. They were sure it was him. I mean, there is no other guy in my life. It had to be him. He's the only one who hangs around me.'

'And did he confess?'

'He kept denying it. And someone shoved him and he fell and his specs broke.' I buried my face in my hands. 'It's all my fault.'

'Don't blame yourself, Divya. I'd called the boys in.'

'They will hate me.'

'They don't actually. They were concerned, protective.'

'And Satish? He's so, so, so nice. He said it was all ok. That he'd help me find this perv.' I am sobbing and I don't even care anymore. Let her see it. I'm not covering my face. She doesn't stop me from crying. She just waits.

'I don't want to talk about that. I feel horrible. I apologized to Satish like a thousand times. We're cool now.'

She asks, 'And what happened at home when your mom found the note?'

'Shit hit the ceiling, didn't it? Er, sorry, Shenaz Miss. I mean, they were both scared and shivering. And blaming each other and then blaming themselves. For not being around. For not knowing their only kid—only kid—one kid—for not knowing she could be killed . . .'

She waits while I blow my nose.

'Divya, I know you won't like this, but I did speak to your parents. It's my job.'

'Your job!' I'm furious, just like that. 'All this is just a job to you. When they find my—my mutilated body— you will say you did your job.'

I stand up again, and this time I'm leaving for good. They're all the same. Adults!

She says, 'We had a really long talk, Divya. Your parents know they've been absent from your life. Emotionally. They were so busy. But they know now. And they're going to try to be there for you. Much more. They want to. Sometimes it takes an incident like this to really wake up to reality perhaps. Their work is important too. But you are more important to them. They'll find a way to balance it out.'

I stand by the chair.

'Okay, Shenaz Miss. I think I'd like to go home now.'

'Divya, wait, we need to decide what to do about your stalker. Is there a need to report him to the police, you think?'

'Not really. I mean he can't harm me if my friends and my parents are around me. Right?' I shrug, but she doesn't look convinced. 'Look, Shenaz Miss, I'll just avoid him, he'll get the message. I am not scared of him anymore.'

'How will you avoid him if you don't know who he is, Divya? Does he no longer want to harm you? What made him change?' Her voice is softer now. I've never heard this tone. She's always loud and screechy during the morning assembly and stuff.

'I don't know, Miss. I think he just loves me and he wanted to help me get noticed. And I have Neeti and the girls and Satish and the other boys to protect me now.'

'And it always feels great to be loved, Divya.' She smiles.

'I—er—I guess so.'

'He made you the centre of attention, right?'

I shuffle. I stare at the pink sky. A flock of birds flies past, together.

I put my hand into my bag and curl my fingers around something. 'He wasn't trying to harm me, Shenaz Miss. He was being helpful. He just came out to show them all that I could—you know—be loved too. I'm not just a blur in the background.' I laugh a bit, like it's another joke.

She nods. 'You're not a blur at all. You're an amazing, intelligent young lady. With a fantastic imagination that will take you places some day'. And then she smiles. It's a warm smile.

'And Shenaz Miss, my parents, ya, he showed them too. You know, like, how easy it would have been for me to have been harmed—while they were looking away. How something dangerous could have happened.'

'Yes,' she says. 'So this follower is not going to bother you any more? No need to tell the police?'

'No. No need to tell my classmates either,' I say, pulling out what I had inside my bag. A green marker pen.

I give it to her. 'Shenaz Miss, he's gone for good. He's become what he saved me from being . . . invisible.'

The Haircut

Andaleeb Wajid

The first time I took a pair of sharp scissors and snipped the ends of my hair, I was thirteen. My mother walked in on me as I sat on the floor of my room, surrounded by newspapers. Ammi's eyes widened and she lost it.

'What are you doing?' she screeched, trying to yank the scissors out of my hand.

'I'm just cutting the split ends,' I told her, holding on to the scissors firmly.

She stopped struggling and sat back on her haunches. 'But why?'

'What do you mean why?'

'What's the need?' she asked. 'In our families, we pride on girls who have long hair.'

I tried not to roll my eyes at her officious tone. I'd heard this enough times to know it verbatim. Girls had to grow their hair out. Very long. I counted down the seconds in my head and right on cue, Ammi spoke.

'A woman's beauty lies in her hair. The longer it is, the more beautiful she is considered.'

By whom, I wanted to ask. Who was this arbiter of beauty who insisted that girls have long hair despite the pains it took to manage said hair? Instead, I sighed.

'Ammi, it's nothing. It's just routine care for my hair,' I said, waiting for her to get up and leave.

'Okay, go ahead and cut it. I want to see.'

I made a face. I wanted privacy, but obviously Ammi had never heard of such a thing. This was why there was no lock on my door, so she could walk in whenever she wanted. But what actually happened was that my unruly brothers—Adnan, Shahid and Bilal—waltzed in and made themselves at home. All the time!

I wrapped my fingers around the thin ends and without realizing it, I looked at her. She shook her head. I lowered my fingers until I was holding on to the very ends of my hair. This time, I didn't look at her as I snipped them off. I could feel her gaze on me, observing my every move, determined to make me rethink my decision. Too late, Ammi.

'Here, give them to me,' she said, taking the tiny lock of hair from my hand. She indicated that I pick the bits of hair that had fallen on the newspaper as well.

'For what?' I asked as I stood up, brushing hair from my clothes.

Ammi made a 'pch' sound as she bent down to collect everything, every last fragment of hair. I looked down at Ammi's own thinning braid. She didn't seem to have taken care of her own hair for some reason. I saw her combing out her hair every morning, wincing whenever she saw how much her hair fell, but she remained impassive. She never really did anything about it.

'It has to be disposed properly. You can't just throw them into the bin. Someone can take it and do jadu-tona with it,' she said seriously.

I stared at her. Had she always been like this? Or had Abbu's death made her into this different person? Someone who was always plagued by what other people would say about us, who would look at her with pity. After all, she was in her thirties with four children to take care of, alone.

I handed her the newspaper with the bits of hair in it and watched Ammi leave, wondering what went on in her head. I knew what went on in mine as I fingered the rough edges, dreaming of smooth rippling hair that I could swish around—the way I had seen women doing it in commercials.

*

I cut my hair again, two years later, for graduation day. It was a big occasion because we all got to wear saris.

Big enough for one of the teachers, Mrs Rajkumar, to repeatedly mortify us with instructions about how we had to wear a bra and that she was appalled that there were some of us who still didn't wear one.

Heera and I giggled at this, briefly checking out each other's chests, but with the double layered uniform it was hard to tell whether we were or not. Not that it mattered. Ours was a girls' school, so our teachers were used to giving us instructions like this, and even telling us what to do if we got our period on graduation day, since we were all going to be wearing white saris.

When graduation day arrived, we reached school in the evening. Parents would be dropping in later for the ceremony. I was jittery and eager and also secretly thrilled because Ammi had given me permission to go to the beauty parlour to get my hair done. She had been too busy doing something else to accompany me, so she sent my older cousin Sumaya apa to be my chaperone. Sumaya apa was both anxious and excited about the responsibility that had befallen her shoulders.

The parlour aunty looked at my hair and sighed.

'Why you girls like such long, long hair, ma?' she asked. She was going to do a French twisty knot and I was eager to see how it would look on me.

I didn't say anything.

'And all these split ends. Can I trim it at least?' she asked.

I shared a look with Sumaya apa in the mirror. Her eyes were wide and she shook her head slightly. Cutting hair was a big no-no in the family unless there was a valid reason for it. But I squared my shoulders and told the lady to trim my hair slightly. It was easier being a rebel when Ammi wasn't around.

'How much?' she asked, holding a healthy fistful of my hair. My stomach contracted with fear at the thought of cutting all that hair away and the kind of *hungama* that awaited me as a result.

'Not that much, aunty!' I squeaked. 'Just a little.' Sumaya apa covered her face in her hands at this point.

Aunty looked disappointed as she let go of my hair and clutched the ends and snipped them in a clean line. Hair fell around me in tiny clumps and I released the breath I had been holding.

Ammi didn't notice anything different about me until nearly three days after graduation. She merely narrowed her eyes and glared after that. She muttered under her breath something about rebellious girls who didn't know any better and would come to a bad end. I wondered what sort of bad end I could possibly come to by cutting my hair? Did she think I'd elope with someone or join the movie industry? Because in her book, a bad end actually meant a bad name for the family. I realize now that as I grew up, I didn't always agree with Ammi or believe in my heart of hearts that

Ammi knew best. In fact, I realized that my mother didn't know much, but I couldn't just go about saying such things to her. So I preferred pretending not to hear her or even acknowledge that she was talking about me.

*

But this time . . . well, this time, I did something different.

I was in the final year of college and we were all buzzing with nervous excitement about the new year. We had career counselling sessions and those who wanted to pursue their masters constantly hounded the teachers for reference letters and other such things. I wasn't sure about what I wanted to do yet. As far as Ammi was concerned, this was the end of the road for me when it came to my education. She had three more children after me to educate, single-handedly. Hoping for more seemed pointless.

One day, I walked into the college to find it abuzz; it was the kind of excitement that usually presided during intercollegiate events or fests where people (read: boys) could come inside our strictly women's only college. I was drifting along in my own dream world, thinking about a troubling conversation I had overheard this morning until I could ignore the din no longer. I walked up to one of the banners hung close by, but Heera dragged me away before I could read what was written on it.

'What's going on?' I asked her as we ambled in the direction of the leafy grove where we often hung out before classes began.

'Some cancer drive or something,' she muttered as she pulled me down beside her, texting furiously.

'He's still acting up?' I asked her, referring to Rishi, her on and off boyfriend of the past two years, who could be really sweet and a complete asshole in the same ten-minute time frame.

'Yeah,' she muttered. She put her phone away and looked up. 'So, what plans for the day?'

'You ask me every day, but you know the answer is always the same,' I told her, rolling my eyes.

'Gah! Why are you such a straight arrow, B?'

I shrugged. I didn't know how to be any other way. Ammi would throw a fit if I told her I wanted to 'hang out' with Heera after college. *But didn't you just spend the entire day with her*, she would ask. Ammi didn't really get the concept of friends, I think. To her, relatives were enough (the horror!).

'You'll make up with Rishi and I'll just be a third wheel, so it's for the best,' I said, putting on a brave face. I had never admitted this to anyone and rarely to myself, but I hated Rishi. I hated him because ever since he swaggered into my friend's life, we never spent any time together, especially during lunchtime, which was supposed to be *our* time. Regular college hours didn't count because we were busy with classes.

Every other day, she ran off to meet him for lunch and it helped that his college was nearby. He was promptly outside our gates in the evenings too, waiting for her. I often gave him the death stare, but he never saw it, let alone acknowledge it, and I never bothered to understand why.

'Ha, fat chance. This time he has to do more than just apologize,' she fumed.

'What happened?' I asked, not sure I wanted to get into her drama while Ammi's plans of getting me married next year reverberated in my ears. I had overheard her talking to someone on the phone earlier. She'd said that finally my education was going to be finished now and she was hoping to get a 'suitable' rishta for me. Not perfect. Not the best. Suitable would do.

I wanted to ask her how she was okay with such a thing. And why was she in such a hurry to get me married? Why did it feel like she was running all the time, with everything that was happening with us? Why couldn't she take a pause and breathe? Why couldn't she let *me* breathe?

But I didn't want to get into a fight with her because that would just end with her in tears about how I was ungrateful and how I never thought about her and how she was bringing up four children alone in the world.

So, listening to Rishi's transgressions wasn't really a priority currently, but I nodded and made appropriate noises before the morning bell rang and we both got up to go to class. Just as I'd predicted, Heera had made up with Rishi before lunch, constantly texting him on her phone under the desk, and she was off for lunch with him somewhere. She was quite excited—he had promised to surprise her with something.

I nodded, hoping my face wouldn't give away my disappointment that I'd be eating lunch all by myself yet again.

But I no longer wanted to sit alone and when one of the girls—Leena, I think—beckoned for me to join her and her group by the huge rain tree, I walked up to them and sat down on the concrete platform around it. Leena was in my class and as usual everyone cracked up over my name when she introduced me to the rest of her friends.

'What does your mother say when she has to call you to come inside? Baahar, andar aao?' a girl called Nita chortled.

'Funny . . .' I said, heat rushing to my face. 'It's not Baahar. It's Bahaar. It means "spring".'

'We know,' someone else said and it felt a wee bit patronizing. But I didn't mind. I just rolled my eyes because this was still better than sitting alone, waiting for Heera to turn up, flushed with excitement with whatever outlandish claims Rishi had made about their future together. Sometimes, I wanted to remind Heera that we were only twenty-one. Not the age to really think about a 'future' with a boyfriend. But then again, I was also the one getting rishtas at twenty-one. So, I wasn't really in a position to speak my mind.

As we passed our lunch boxes around, I heard everyone discussing the event that was taking place today. It was a hair donation drive for cancer patients!

The spoon in my hand froze mid-air.

'Hair donation?' I asked.

Nita nodded as she twirled her shoulder-length hair around. 'I wish I had longer hair. I could have donated some.'

'Your mother won't say anything?'

The words slipped out of my mouth before I could stop myself. I often forgot that not everyone's mother was like mine.

'Oh, she will, but she'll get over it. Anyway, if I cut this any shorter, I might have to go bald and *then* we'll have the apocalypse on our hands,' she grinned, her hair swaying ever so slightly. Perfectly.

I listened to the others in silence and quietly told myself to stop thinking about it. There was no way I could justify donating my hair to Ammi. But everyone had started commenting on each other's hair and Leena gasped when she saw mine.

'Look! Bahaar's hair falls nearly to her waist! They could make so many wigs out of this!'

I smiled uneasily. 'I can't cut my hair,' I said quickly.

'Why? Is it against your religion?' another girl asked me curiously. I shook my head.

'No, but . . .'

'Then it's for a good cause, right?'

'Yes, but . . .'

'Let her be. Don't force her to do something she doesn't want to,' Nita said with a smile. I smiled back at her, aware that she had just saved me from unnecessary arguments, but also annoyed that she had stepped in like some sort of saviour.

I didn't need saving.

We all finished our lunch, but stayed there chatting. My eyes kept straying to the banner nearest us.

Don't. Even. Think. Of. It. Bahaar.

I dusted my salwar as I stood up and dropped my empty tiffin box into my backpack. Should I head back to class or hang around here, waiting for Heera to show up, I wondered. How pathetic, I told myself. Did I have no life outside of being her friend?

Even as I stood there, mulling over what to do next, Nita bumped my shoulder with hers. 'Come on. Let's go check it out,' she said.

'What?' I asked, surprised. Nita was one of the most popular girls in college and I was both appalled and excited that she wanted to hang out with me, even though I'd felt resentful towards her just minutes ago.

'That hair donation drive thingy,' she explained.

'No, I don't want to,' I said quickly.

'We're just going to see it,' she promised as she dragged me away with her. I followed her and some other girls to the tent that had been set up near the quadrangle of the college. A woman stood at the entrance of the tent, handing out flyers and there was a standee outside it, explaining what was going on.

We hung around, watching a few girls go inside, looking curious but also slightly apprehensive. But the buzz there had been this morning (which could have been because it was a change from routine and not because it was actually something exciting) was now sorely lacking.

We read the flyer that explained how and what would be done with the hair they collected. They would make them into wigs for cancer patients who had lost their hair due to chemotherapy and for each wig, they needed hair from at least six women. My eyebrows shot up. That was a LOT of hair.

Hair was such a strange thing. My mother said it was the mark of my beauty, but no one else was allowed to see it. So who was the beauty for, Ammi? And if my hair helped someone else feel even a little good or positive about themselves, what was the harm in that?

We wanted to see what the girls who had donated their hair looked like when they came outside, but the bell for the next class rang and we had to leave. I didn't realize I was clutching the flyer in my hand as I walked back to class.

As expected, Heera was over the moon with whatever gifts Rishi had given her and was whispering to me constantly about what an excellent kisser he was. Ugh. Not that I looked down on kissing as such, or even the two of them kissing. But I wasn't interested in the details, please.

I excused myself to go to the restroom and walked out of the class. But my feet seemed to be leading me towards the hair donation tent. It was empty now, except for the people who were part of the organization conducting the drive.

'Hi!' a young girl said brightly.

'Hi,' I replied uncertainly. Why was I here? What did I hope to accomplish? *Turn around. Go back*, a voice whispered in my head.

'Shouldn't you be in class?' one of the older women asked. I shook my head.

'I have a free period,' I lied.

'So, are you here to donate your hair?' the young girl asked, walking around me in a circle to inspect my hair, which was hanging down my back in a long braid.

I looked around—the tent was lit by a tube light sort of thing they had rigged up somewhere. There was a large mirror propped up on a stand and before it, there was a stool. On a table nearby, scissors gleamed.

Don't do it, the voice in my head screamed. I looked at the young girl instead and said, 'Yes'.

I realized that classes were still going on when I walked out of the tent. But I couldn't go back in the middle of a lecture like this. So I stuck around outside, waiting near one of the trees for the teacher to leave. I could sneak in before the next teacher came.

But then, everyone would look at me, I thought frantically. And with that realization came the swift and hot feeling that Ammi was probably going to scalp me alive for doing this. What had I done? I hadn't even looked at myself in the mirror after they had cut the requisite 12 inches. The young girl, who introduced herself as Sara, styled it and said my hair framed my face in a really nice way. But I was too scared to look.

I didn't return to class at all. If I had my bag with me, I could have snuck out from college once the evening bell had rung, but my bag was still in the classroom and it had my phone in it. I was half glad my phone wasn't with me or I'd have been inundated with messages from Heera asking where I was. Once she noticed my absence, of course.

When I saw girls streaming out of the building, I waited for everyone to leave. I hadn't seen Heera leave, but she must have been in that huge group that had converged towards the gates. So I quickly ran upstairs to grab my bag when a gasp stopped me on the landing.

'What have you done?'

It was Heera, holding my bag in her hands.

'I . . .'

Nita was coming down the stairs after her and she looked at me and grinned widely.

'Oh my God, you did it!'

Heera turned to her, as though surprised I knew Nita. I shrugged at both of them and took my bag from Heera without a word.

'Why did you do it? What's wrong with you?' Heera asked in a loud whisper.

I saw Nita's frown, but I didn't want her to intercede on my behalf yet again, so I shook my head. 'It was for a good cause. The hair will be made into wigs for cancer patients.'

Heera looked like she wanted to say more, but she dragged me out with her.

'You look nice!' Nita called out and left with a wave of her hand and I followed Heera to the gate.

'But dude, your *mom*,' she said. 'Won't she kill you?'

I nodded. Or something close. But I'd done it and there was no going back.

Rishi was waiting for Heera at the gate, no surprises there, but he glanced at me and did a double take.

'Who's *this*?' he asked. Heera looked at him incredulously, but didn't say anything as she walked off in a huff. I wasn't sure who she was irritated with, me or him.

I got an auto and sat inside, dread clutching my insides. To say that I was afraid of Ammi's reaction was an understatement. I thought of the different ways Ammi would want to kill me.

I was in a dilemma as I entered the house. I wanted her to be done with me quickly, but I also didn't want to be discovered at the same time. As I walked inside, I heard voices, making my anxiety flare up even more. We had guests at home today? Of all days? No, no, no! I thought of the possible excuses I could make—my hair got entangled in a passing scooter's handles and they had to cut it off to save my life—I slipped and fell in some cow dung (strategically so that it got only on my hair and not on my clothes) and it was stinking so much that I had to cut it off—but I knew that Ammi wouldn't buy any of it.

'Here she comes,' Ammi said warmly. I winced. Who had come home? Why couldn't Ammi have called and told me in advance?

I quickly wrapped my dupatta around my head like a hijab and walked into the hall where Ammi was talking to a few aunties who looked at me with a great deal of interest.

I smiled and nodded to them and hoped that Ammi didn't expect me to stick around and make small talk. So far, no one had noticed anything. Ammi had barely glanced at me. My twelve-year-old brother, Bilal, the youngest and brattiest, came barrelling through the door and clung to my side, tugging at my kurta. Ammi looked at him in exasperation. We were all tired of his antics, but he had become more and more unmanageable as the years passed and Ammi rued that it was because of the absence of a male figure in the house. Eyeroll.

'So when is her education getting completed?' one of the aunties asked, glancing at me.

'This year. She has her final exams in May,' Ammi replied.

'You know this is actually a good idea. Our Hashim will be returning from Dubai in July. We can fix the engagement and . . .' the aunty paused, looking at the expression on my face.

I looked at them in horror as my brother playfully tugged at my dupatta. I tried to hold on to it, to preserve this idea of normalcy, wondering why I was so shocked at what the lady had said when I had been expecting this to happen all along. But today, a part of me decided to let go. Maybe Ammi doesn't know what's best, after all.

The dupatta slipped from my head, making my hair sway dramatically, just like the commercials. The women stared at me, waiting for me to say something. But I only looked at Ammi, who glared back at me in deathly silence.

The Crip Gang

Anusha Misra

Before you read my story, please know that I've accepted who I am, partly, if not completely. I'm Nu, aged twenty-two, queer, chaotic and disabled. I love the colour baby pink and I have light blue hair. Oh, and I walk with a crutch. Most people's first reaction when I say this has been, 'Oh, I'm so sorry to hear that.' But that's what this story is about. To tell you about how I found joy and belonging in my disabled experience while living in a world where most stories are about able-bodied men and women enjoying, dancing and succeeding while the disabled character struggles their entire life only to be called 'inspirational'.

Don't get me wrong, disability goes hand in hand with a struggle: an internal struggle with the outside world, a struggle to be independent, a struggle to 'prove everyone wrong', a struggle to set boundaries with people, a struggle to exist. Growing up, my history teacher would read out great stories of able-bodied men conquering great cities, my literature teacher would tell me about able-bodied Rosalind and Orlando falling in love, while I would try to draw perfectly circular arcs in geometry. 'No uneven, crooked lines,' my maths teacher would shout.

The journey to being kinder to myself started in the summer of 2017, when I moved to Delhi for college. It's a story of four disabled women who taught me how to accept my identity: Ahalya, Minn, Ina and of course, Nu! (I played a big role in accepting myself too.)

College was a terrifying idea because, suddenly, I had all the freedom in the world; freedom from my childhood. You see, I'd never felt like there was a space where I belonged—where I could be myself. My entire life, I've felt like I'm too short, too anxious, too quiet, too small to truly take up space—in simple terms, too disabled. And I spent a lot of time 'compensating' for my disability. People who are discriminated against their entire lives start believing they deserve a lot of the things they go through, because that's the only reality they've ever known. I grew up with relatives telling me that I had a stroke and couldn't walk because I must have done a very bad deed in my previous life. I was cursed and I believed them.

When I moved from Kolkata to Delhi, I was terrified of living alone—mostly because of what everyone had to say about me living alone (unsolicited opinions from people who never truly knew me) like:

Concerned aunty (who last met me when I was ten) to my most supportive mother: *'How will she manage alone, Mayura? She has lived with you for the past nineteen years! How can you let her go?'*

And as a physically disabled individual with a mental illness, I've had to fight constantly. Fight the world, fight my body to function better, fight discrimination, fight a society that is not logistically designed to accommodate my disabled body.

Before I continue, I should give you a bit of a backstory: I had a stroke at nine years of age due to a chronic illness called lupus (Look it up, Selena Gomez has it too!). The stroke affected my mobility and I turned from an able-bodied individual to a disabled individual. Thus began an uphill climb of redefining my world view and reclaiming life according to my needs and convenience.

That didn't happen for the longest time because acceptance is definitely not a linear path. It is rather a scribble from one end of the paper to another. It took me several years to be proud of my disability and of myself. Disabled teenagers, like me, grew up disliking the bodies we grew up in. We saw our body as an instrument that held us back, that prevented us from doing all the things we saw our able-bodied friends doing.

I went to a school where I never encountered anyone with visible differences or anyone who used a mobility aid. I grew up around able-bodied classmates who couldn't help but treat me differently. I was excluded from conversations about dating and all PG-13 stuff. I grew up around able-bodied ideals of competition, productivity, time, independence. Meanwhile, as I'd look down at my crooked, bent fingers that begged for my love and acceptance, I quickly learnt to hide them under my coat. It was apparently 'unattractive' and 'hideous' to be disabled. I grew up listening to fairy tales where only witches have crooked teeth, crooked fingers, crooked legs. Meanwhile, Cinderella is able-bodied, tall and white.

College was the first time I ever had classmates with disabilities and it warmed my heart. I heaved a sigh of relief because all this while, I had a certain fear that I was all alone in an able-bodied world. I was obsessed with showing others that I wasn't disabled. At the airport, I would ask for a wheelchair because the walk across that vast space exhausted me. But over time, I noticed that people would stare (as people always do) at my hands and legs when I was in the wheelchair. So, to show them that I wasn't like the 'typical disabled person', I would cross my legs because according to a young me, disabled people couldn't cross their legs. I was, clearly, generalizing. I had an urge to dress 'cooler' than a 'typical' disabled person because I thought disabled folks would dress drab and be utterly boring instead of someone who had a wonderful personality. I believed that all the interesting people were able-bodied because it's all I knew.

It might sound illogical now, but my anxiety made this seem so rational at the time. I feel like I've always had the fear of people looking at me. I've been intimidated by people's eyes. When I look at a person, the first thing I notice are their eyes because they're usually staring at my legs and the next thing I know, they're being intrusive and asking me questions about my illness.

Things changed in my second year of college. I was the quietest girl in class because I was too afraid to speak up. My speech disability made me hate my voice. I was afraid to say, 'Present, ma'am!' and announce my existence to the class. I was petrified of talking to my other classmates because I always imagined their puzzled faces when I attempted to say something. So I stopped putting effort into socializing.

*

Ina was the second quietest girl in class. She joined us in second year when she transferred from her college to mine. Ina first approached me when I was sitting under the peepul tree (alone) and eating my lunch. She waved but didn't say anything. I waved back and continued eating my lunch, wondering why the second quietest girl in my class was approaching me. Then she took both of her hands and signalled to her ear and mouth and started mumbling something incomprehensible. 'I'm sorry, what?' I said, puzzled. She signalled to my phone and began typing something on hers. All of a sudden, my phone vibrated. It was a message from her! It said:

Hello, I'm Ina. I'm deaf and that's why I was signalling to my ear and mouth. Hope I didn't creep you out! I noticed you don't talk to anyone in class and neither do I! They don't understand me. Do you want to be friends?

To say I was excited was an understatement. Had I finally found someone whom I identified with, who didn't make me feel completely lost in this able-bodied world of my college? Or rather had she found me? How would I communicate with Ina? I'd always wondered if people would accept me for who I was. I had been told that I sounded like I was 'ill'. Some directly dismissed what I had to say, saying that they didn't understand me at all (and would give up making any efforts to do so). I was a volcano waiting to erupt. I had so much to say and yet something was holding me back.

Ina and I ate lunch together from then on. We didn't talk, but would occasionally smile at each other. I didn't know anything about sign language. I didn't even know anything about fellow disabled folks! Suddenly, I felt very guilty about alienating my own community, except at that point I never called it *my* community. It still felt pretty alien to me, but after meeting Ina, I began to identify as disabled. It felt nice to finally have a sense of belonging in this great big city, even if it was a speck.

I never had to hide my disability from Ina. She knew the real me, anxiety, speech disability, crutch and all. You see, my relationship with my crutch was a complicated one. I would often hide my crutch behind my back whenever I was in a group photo, so that strangers viewing the photo wouldn't notice the awkward girl with the crutch. I used to carry my crutch in my left arm and my bag on the other when I walked to my hostel because the road was coarse and covered with pebbles. Once, when I was rushing for class, I tripped and bruised my knee because I was walking without my crutch, which only slowed me down. I had always thought of my crutch as an inconvenience rather than an aid that made my life easier.

In reality, my crutch had taken me on so many different adventures. We should also see the flip side: Being disabled is so exciting! Every day for a disabled person is an adventure. After meeting Ina, I slowly started imagining my walk back to the hostel as a game of Temple Run. There were many hurdles to overcome, decisions to make, paths to take.

Over the course of my years in college, when my interactions with folks from the community increased, I realized that I was not stranded alone in the middle of a world that was not made for me. I came to discover that self-love comes the hard way and I was still a student in that realm. But I'm getting ahead of myself.

I only accepted a tiny bit of myself when I met Ina, the part of me that disliked my speech. Seeing another person with the same struggles as mine gave me confidence to speak up. I even went to my first Equal Opportunities Society meeting with Ina. And that is where I met Ahalya.

Ahalya was the president of this society, a place I was hesitant to join at the beginning of college. I wanted nothing to do with disabled people even though I was a part of that existence. I was denying myself my own reality. I turned the other way when the disabled club of my college would call me for meetings. Such a reaction is often very common for marginalized folks who've denied themselves their own realities because we've been taught to dislike our bodies.

Ahalya was curious, wide-eyed and had a certain sparkle in her eyes as she chattered. She was an amputee and often used the phrase, *'Meri ek taang nakli hai!'* (I have a fake limb). She had decorated her prosthetic with flowers and painted it pink. My eyes went wide with curiosity. 'Oh, you can do that? How'd I never thought of this before!' I asked myself. When I saw others loving their mobility aids, I learned how to be kinder to my own too.

Ahalya had been fighting to make our college accessible for years. Our new administration had become stricter about their security policies, and some of them discriminated against disabled folk in the college. For example, vehicles weren't allowed to enter within campus and many like me often had to walk a long distance to the hostel. Ahalya and the other coordinators of the society had made petitions and succeeded in building ramps as a start. But accessibility doesn't only end with accessible physical spaces. It also lies in the minds and eyes of those who attempt to understand our realities and look at things from our perspective. Unfortunately, the administration always needed a bit of a reminder that we didn't need to be pitied but instead heard and thought of.

I was very aware that I was pitied; I saw it in my classmates' eyes, in the eyes of the library head who was talking to the person standing beside him. I heard them in earshot. 'Oh no, look at her, she has to suffer so much,' they say while clicking their tongues. Let me ask you, why do we choose only to see one part of the disabled experience? The one with all the medical procedures and the suffering. Why does sad background music always play when a disabled character comes on-screen or describes their journey? Why can't kids just be taught that different bodies have different needs instead? If I'm being honest, before I went to college, I didn't even know I was allowed to ask for accessibility. Accessibility in the world is so scarce that many unaware disabled folk often feel like they need to just adjust to an inaccessible world. There's no other way.

Now that I was living alone in a new city, I had to book my own therapist appointments, learn how to be kinder to myself, how to make the right decisions, teach myself to work harder because we live in a world where disabled folk constantly need to prove themselves. I lived in a small, cramped hostel room, one that couldn't accommodate wheelchair users. When I entered the hostel premises for the first time, there was no ramp to go to the quadrangle. I often had to get help to go up and down the stairs. I no longer had Mom to help me tie my hair or attach the hooks of my earrings because I couldn't attach them myself due to my disabled left hand (petition for accessible earrings, by the way). I learned to ask for help from my hostel mates over the years. I had grown up thinking that my disability made me inferior, weak and asking for help would simply tarnish my reputation as I was already a burden by being around people. One of the realizations I've reached, over the years, is that it is absolutely okay to ask for help, even if it's a simple thing such as wearing a complicated gown or attaching hooks at the back of a dress.

Minn ushered herself into my room one cold Delhi afternoon in search of a mop. She lived in the hostel, in the room across from mine, in room 40. I had always observed her from afar until then. I would listen to her talk animatedly to everyone, always cheerful, always loud, 'too loud', I thought to myself. But she looked shorter and smaller in person with her right hand hidden under her coat. She picked up the mop with her left hand, right hand still hidden. This reminded me of how insecure I was of my own disabled left hand, how I would always keep it hidden under the shadow of my right, though I still didn't know why Minn kept her hand hidden. As she was exiting my room, she suddenly turned and smiled at me and said, 'Hi, I think we haven't really spoken even though we live across from each other! Do you want to come to my room?'

I took a moment to take it all in before saying, 'Hi, sure, I'll come to your room after dinner!'

I went for a walk with Minn that night, a first for me (to walk at night and to walk with a friend) ever since I took admission. I could call her a friend, and not an acquaintance because that night, as we walked, she told me things that only a friend would tell the other. She told me the story of her hidden right hand, and it was then that I realized that her right hand was just like my left hand. I realized then that I had been so afraid of my left hand my entire life and had made sure my lines were straight because that was the norm. Minn showed me how to embrace messy lines, just like her curly hair and love the unconventional and strange. Minn taught me how to love my hands.

As four disabled folks living away from home, Ina, Ahalya, Minn and I learnt to adjust to an inaccessible world together. As women with mobility aids, we could never be spontaneous. We had to think a thousand times before we ordered an Uber, before we stepped out of the hostel, before we entered a marketplace. As disabled young adults, we started learning how to love ourselves. We were finally, finally doing things, simply *being* those women we'd always wanted to be. Twelve-year-old Nu had always hoped to go out and live in a new city, all by herself. She prayed to learn to accept herself and simply to *be* by herself. To take up space in her own way. And perhaps a boyfriend wouldn't hurt either, you know?

As disabled folks, we have plenty of firsts in our lives as adults; first time wearing our shoes, tying laces, doing our hair, all by ourselves. We start from scratch again and again, retraining our brain to perform everyday activities that most take for granted. Ina made me realize that we should celebrate every small occasion, however simple it may be. She would buy me my favourite chocolate from the canteen whenever I stood in a line for more than five minutes (I hated standing in lines because it gave me intense, *crippling* anxiety, pun intended). We would go out to celebrate whenever Ahalya managed to finally get through to the principal to sign our listicle for a more accessible college and whenever Minn 'unhid' her right hand from her undercoat for an entire day.

We began to call ourselves 'The Crip Gang' because we wanted to reclaim the word 'cripple'. The Crip Gang had a motto to 'Unhide the Disability' and overthrow ableism. Word soon spread around the college, and wherever you looked, in every nook and corner of the college, you would find the four of us: whether it was the amphitheatre, the benches next to the lawn or the shade under the canteen. We had elaborate discussions on discrimination, dating, defining our identity. We used to have tiny dance parties in Minn's room.

We would somehow sneak in Ahalya and Ina (who were day scholars and strictly not allowed in the hostel) into our room during lunchtime. After our successful mission of sneaking them in, we would make the room as accessible as possible and remove all the furniture that might make us trip, close the curtains, turn on the music and dance with abandon.

Now when I look back, I feel like college was a source of freedom for so many of us, disabled or able-bodied—we were no longer within the four walls of our school, we were no longer under parental supervision. Sometimes, it was overwhelming, but we learnt how to strike a balance.

Ahalya was the boldest among us. Whenever we went out as a group, Ahalya was the only one who had the guts to go up to the stranger staring at us and say, 'Is there a problem?' I admired her grit but at the same time, I was afraid. I was afraid because we as women have always been taught to be afraid. That doesn't change, disabled or not. My mother was terrified when I told her that I'd be going out with my friends for the evening. Ahalya taught me how to fight and to confront people. She had fought her whole life: fought for equal rights as a disabled person, fought to create an accessible college, fought the canteen bhaiya whenever her spicy honey fries got delayed and she had to rush for her society meeting, fought her family that told her that her disability made her weak and she wouldn't be able to manage in college.

There's always a certain kind of extra pressure on disabled women to prove the world wrong, to prove to them that we aren't weak or just worthy of inspiration. I'm not going to beat around the bush. There are good days and bad, when one is disabled. Being disabled in college is hard. But with Ina, Minn and Ahalya by my side, I felt like there wasn't anything I couldn't do.

The first time Minn went on a date, we were all very excited. Minn, in typical Minn fashion, described the date as awkward, storybook-ish, a fairytale. She told us how he came to pick her up in his car and as he opened the door for her, she froze in her steps. What followed were awkward glances, Minn tucking in her right hand further into her fur coat and looking down at her feet. This continued for a minute and took place all too quickly, in no particular order. Minn simply froze because he opened the car door for her and she considered this an other-worldly grand gesture. Eventually, as she hopped on over to his car, they laughed about it. When Minn returned, she couldn't help but gush about her lovely date with 'the first guy who picked her up in his car'.

In the past, Minn told us, she had dated men who often told her things like, 'Oh, you're too pretty to be disabled!' or 'My girlfriend can't be disabled.'

An unaware Minn, in such moments, had taken it as a compliment. But eventually, she realized that ableism often manifests itself in the form of compliments.

As Minn started talking about love, all of us began thinking. All our lives we'd perceived love to be terrifying and inaccessible. All of us had grown up watching able-bodied men and women fall in love on-screen. As children who are young and impressionable, we begin to pick up an ideal form of femininity from the world around us: this is how men and women are supposed to behave. Women are taught from a very young age that they're considered worthy only if they have a significant other and they settle down. Women are supposed to accept the destiny that patriarchy has carved out for them. While able-bodied women are supposed to accept their roles as mothers and caregivers, disabled women are stripped off their roles of motherhood and caregiving because folks don't expect us to take care of others, or ourselves for that matter. We aren't expected to dress up, put on lipstick or fall in love.

I distinctly remember how our hostel warden would always point at me and Minn and ask us, (while her spectacles were atop her nose, a comical sight): '*Lipstick lagake kaha jaa rahi ho tum dono?*' (*Why are you so dressed up, with lipstick and all? Where are you going?*)

Together and apart, Ina, Ahalya, Minn and I learnt to carve out our own ideal, an ideal that made us happy.

We fell in love, had our hearts broken, learnt our lessons. All of us went with Ina to get her nose pierced. As we looked over at her worriedly, she chuckled as her nose got pricked. We all got tattoos of our mobility aids. While Ina had a hearing aid as a miniature tattoo with 'CG' (Crip Gang) written below, I had a tattoo of a crutch, Ahalya had a tattoo of a prosthetic leg and Minn had a tattoo of her curled up disabled left hand. As we started to explore *Nayi Dilli* together, we started to own our narrative.

Although, this doesn't mean we lived happily ever after. This isn't an end just because all four of us accepted our disabilities and ourselves. Sometimes, I would wake up frustrated on a winter morning that I couldn't get out of bed immediately and walk to the bathroom because my limbs were so stiff. I often had to call my roommate to help me up. This made me ashamed sometimes, because I hated asking for any kind of help from anyone and exposing my weakness. Ina still got frustrated when no one heard what she had to say in class; after all, just because Ina communicated differently than others didn't mean she had nothing *valuable* to say. Minn would still hide her hand from the boy she liked until she felt like she knew him enough to tell him about her disability. Ahalya was Ahalya: she was always the life of the party, always happy, always smiling. But after I got to know her better,

she told me that she only cried within the confines
of her room because she was once shamed for being
vulnerable when she was just a child. Her body was
still getting used to a prosthetic and to a leg that was
no longer there—and that was very painful, the kind
of throbbing pain that couldn't be ignored. All of us
learnt to deal with loneliness, with mood swings and
anger; it's almost like we were discovering new things
about ourselves every day. After all, we had to be our
own parents now that we were living alone.

Acceptance was, unfortunately, not just a one-time
affair. It was and still is a process for the four of us.
After all, we are the only ones who have to live with
ourselves our entire lives and this is why it matters to
most. We don't care what others think of us but only
what we think of ourselves and neither should anyone
else, disabled or not. Trust me, I know what I'm talking
about—I smash ableism for a living!

Note: This story didn't actually happen. Nu didn't have the much-needed support system that we all crave in college. As a disabled woman, Nu has found friendships and relationships inaccessible her entire life. She's always felt like she had to work hard for others' affection and that somehow, she wasn't adequate enough. Many of us feel lost and invisible in college. We don't get the perfect group of friends, like they show in movies. So many of us feel otherized and excluded. This otherization has existed for Nu wherever she went: as it often does, for other disabled people like her.

So what can we do to stop the otherization and exclusion of our disabled friends in colleges? For a brief moment, imagine Nu, Ina, Minn and Ahalya in your school/college. All of us have different bodies. Some are tall, some are short, some are fat, some are skinny. Some of us have different kinds of arms and legs. Some have stretch marks on their knees while some have pimples on their faces. Nu would often paint beautiful clouds on her scars as a form of warmth and self-care. What would you like to paint on your scars? Is your body a hotel you regularly check in and out of, or is it a home you can always come back to?

This story is filled with terms that many of you might have learned for the first time today. Here is a small guide to help you get started.

\#   **Mobility Aids**: Remember that we navigate
     through our environment in different ways too!
     Just like Nu uses a crutch to walk (pink-coloured
     crutches are her favourite!), Ina requires a hearing
     aid to communicate with her friends and the people
     around her. All of us require help to survive and
     thrive in the world. This doesn't make us weak or
     undeserving. Or rather, something spectacular. It's
     simply ordinary. Wheelchairs, crutches and hearing
     aids are called mobility aids. They make the Crip
     Gang's life easier. It is alright to use a mobility
     aid. It's completely commonplace, in fact. If you
     have a friend who uses a wheelchair, or walks with
     a crutch, or uses a hearing aid, you are allowed
     to politely ask them about it. You are allowed to
     be curious about it. But when you make a new
     friend who uses a mobility aid, and you're having
     a conversation, be mindful of the questions you
     ask them. All questions shouldn't be related to why
     they might be on a wheelchair because, after all,
     that isn't the only interesting thing about them,
     right?

\#   **Disabled**: Ina, Minn, Nu and Ahalya are disabled—
     and they proudly agree. While Ina was born deaf,
     Ahalya lost her leg in an accident, Minn has a
     disability called cerebral palsy and Nu had a brain

stroke and so she had to learn how to walk again, talk again, paint again, love again. Just a minor setback, no biggie. Her mother used to call her stroke *a second childhood*. Ina, Minn, Ahalya and Nu are a group that knows themselves and their own needs. They get to define their own disability or whether they'd like to call themselves disabled, because it's their own identity! 'Disabled' is definitely not a bad or a harsh word. In my opinion, it's better to use the term 'disabled' than 'differently abled' because the disabled community and the able-bodied (non-disabled) community are vastly different, which is absolutely all right. The two communities have their own unique identity and shouldn't be mixed up. 'Disabled' is a word that is to the point—it doesn't beat around the bush, it doesn't sugar-coat disability. Even so, it is the choice of the person with a disability what they prefer to be addressed as. Ask them how they'd like to be addressed.

Able-bodied: Folks who are not disabled, are called able-bodied or non-disabled. It is our duty to bridge the gap between the disabled and able-bodied communities. Go and hug your disabled friends! One more thing: disabled narratives are not meant to inspire, comfort or please able-bodied folk. Disabled folks write our stories for ourselves:

to understand our disabled identities better and to find home within ourselves. In fact, that's why Nu wrote this story!

Ableism: When someone thinks differently about another person just because they're different, it's called prejudice. A kind of prejudice is ableism, where disabled folks are treated differently (mostly in a negative way) than able-bodied folks. Always remember, it's not the disability that makes us disabled, but ableism in our environment in the form of inaccessibility.

Remember the part before Nu left to pursue her graduation in Delhi where folks would ask her mother questions like, 'How will she manage alone in Delhi? Who will take care of her?' This is a classic example of ableism: doubting Nu's ability to take care of her own self because she's disabled.

Another example of ableism is when men who dated Minn would tell her, 'Oh, you're too pretty to be disabled!' Such a comment is erasing our disabled experience. Disability was a part of the Crip Gang's life; yes, it wasn't the only part, but it was very much a prominent part. And there is no shame in admitting that.

\#   **Accessibility**: This is a concept that makes a disabled person's life easier. The ramps that you see at movie halls, at schools, they all make it easier for us to access places. Accessibility doesn't come easily to everyone—if you were able to climb stairs easily, would you think about a ramp? Now imagine yourself in a scenario where you get a fracture due to an accident and are unable to climb stairs. In such a case, a ramp or a lift would make life much easier for you.

Remember, each story is equally important and all of them matter. If your parent or guardian shuns the topic of disability, remind them that disability is not a bad thing and doesn't deserve to be ignored. It deserves to be discussed. We need to start a conversation and acknowledge the existence of disabled folk. We need more disabled scientists, more disabled teachers, more disabled storytellers. We need a Crip Revolution!

Dropping the Act

Kautuk Srivastava

The shrill shriek of the bell rang through the halls and corridors of Swami Sachdev College. In class S-21, the professor of film studies stopped mid-sentence, let out a sigh and ambled out. *How does every batch get worse than the one before it,* she thought to herself, shaking her head, as if that gesture would rid her of the memories of the disinterested students, the uncontrollable flirting between hormonal adolescents and the constant interjections of that king of brats, Udayan Sinha.

She couldn't get through two sentences without that Udayan squeaking in a smart-ass comment that made the class explode in laughter. She had seen enough class clowns in her twelve years at the college, but Udayan frightened her because he was proof that the class clown species was mutating. Unlike the variety of clowns that had populated classes so far, Udayan wasn't a backbencher, nor was he academically backward.

On the contrary, he had topped the previous semester and he regularly occupied the bench closest to the board, where his eager eyes and silly grin were on full display.

The professor of film studies shuddered to think of what that pest must be up to, now that she had vacated the classroom.

The next lecture for the first year mass media students of Swami Sachdev College was effective communication skills, which was taught by Professor Shirodkar, a short man with several distinct mannerisms that always tickled the students. And as the class waited for the professor to amble his way to the classroom, Udayan, at the goading of the entire batch, had made his way to the front of the class.

He had snatched a pair of spectacles from a nearby student and planted it as low on his nose as possible without obstructing his airflow. He barrelled out his chest and patted his vertical wall of hair into a rigid side parting. And though he was a teenager in a baggy T-shirt and low-hanging jeans, when he mimed patting an imaginary moustache, it seemed to the entire class that he was indeed the stern, stickler that was Professor Shirodkar.

'Yeeeessss, keeeeeds,' shrieked Udayan, peeling back his cheeks in an accurate rendition of the professor's voice and delivery, 'Anyone have the doubt?'

The class doubled over with laughter. They slammed desks and clung to each other. Just the sight of a boy channelling the spirit of a forty-five-year-old teacher seemed to make them shake with joy. Standing alone in front of the whiteboard, Udayan soaked in the attention. It was euphoric and powerful to be able to make a roomful of people react just the way he wanted them to. As their decibels rose, so did the energy of his performance. Soon, he began berating them, 'Stop laugheeng! STOP LAUGHEEEEEENG!' The more he said that, the harder they convulsed.

Lost in character, he didn't notice the square frame of Professor Shirodkar glide into class. He didn't feel the professor's silent glare lock on him. All he noticed was the abrupt drop in enthusiasm from his audience. 'What happeeeeeened?' he screeched.

No one laughed. Some of them shook their heads. Some averted their gaze. He saw a few eyeballs leap to the right of him. Udayan turned slowly and saw the heavy-breathing professor.

Then the professor said, 'How do you like my meeemeecreeeee? HAAN?!'

The class sat up straight, jolted by the ferocity of the professor. Udayan gulped. He looked into the savage, unblinking eyes of Mr Shirodkar. Then against his better instincts, he blurted out, 'The voice is fine, but you should work on the acting.'

Yet again, against their will, the class broke into fitful titters, leading Professor Shirodkar to give them an excellent impression of an angry professor chasing a student out of a classroom.

*

Sitting in the canteen, Udayan was lazily swirling a noodle around his fork when the classes broke for recess. He texted his closest buddy in the BMM department—Siddharth Bhosle—to join him. A few minutes later, Siddharth plodded wearily into the canteen and settled into the chair opposite Udayan with a sigh, grabbing the second fork and picking at the noodles.

'Good, you got kicked out. Damn boring lecture,' said Siddharth.

'Man, he was pissed today', said Udayan. 'I thought he was going to hit me.'

'You deserved it though.'

'What do you mean?'

'I thought you went a little too far. Poor guy. He seemed hurt.'

'Put the fork down,' commanded Udayan. 'If you're on Shirodkar's side, then go steal noodles from his plate only.'

'Arre, I enjoyed it. I just felt like you ragged him too much,' said Siddharth while dumping a clump of angry red schezwan sauce on to a patch of noodles.

'You don't understand comedy, Sid. You think I hurt Shirodkar. But I don't look at it like that. I think I entertained the entire class. Mathematically, which is better? One Shirodkar feeling bad or sixty students feeling good?'

'Yeah . . . I guess that makes sense.'

Just then, there came a loud crash, which was followed by a flurry of raised, angry men's voices. They seemed to come from a distance. The angry voices stilled the conversation in the canteen. Siddharth and Udayan stared at each other wide-eyed.

Then in a hushed, excited whisper, Udayan said, 'Come, let's see.'

He sprang from his chair, without sparing a second thought for the Triple Schezwan he was leaving behind. He tore through the quadrangle, following the angry voices. Siddharth huffed behind him. He arrived at the main gate of the college to see a crowd gathered all around it. He pushed his way through and finally saw the beating heart of the chaos.

A gang of five men were demolishing Shankar Juice Centre. The little tin board lay limp on the pavement. While one man stomped on it vigorously, another flung glasses to the floor, which shattered with a shimmering crash. Glass shards flew everywhere. At one point, he flung a glass too close to the man stomping on the sign, who jumped back and rebuked the glass-flinger.

Two more men were diligently upturning the chairs and tables and hurling fruits out of the tiny shop. A fifth, and the biggest of the lot, stood in front of the carnage, daring someone to intervene. And poor Shankar stood beside the fifth man, begging him to end the wrecking. He winced each time a glass broke and his body drooped as the marauders ransacked his shop. No one said a word. There must have been a hundred people lining the footpaths, but the only voices that could be heard were those of the angry men who shouted a chant as they went about their destruction.

Suddenly, a familiar voice spoke in Udayan's ear, 'You shouldn't be here.' Udayan turned and saw terror mapping Siddharth's face.

'Why?' he whispered back.

'Because—you idiot—you're from Bihar.'

'So?'

'So?! They're from the MPP. They are against Biharis.'

As Siddharth said this, Udayan noticed the clothes the men were wearing. They all had orange T-shirts on. Painted on the back, in big bold Devanagari script was written the name of the party: Maharashtra Pragati Party. Suddenly, he could hear the Bihari lilt in Shankar's plaintive voice as he appealed to the men to stop.

Then, the fifth man addressed Shankar.

'Twice I have asked you to change your shop board to Marathi. Then why you didn't do?'

Shankar tried to reply, but the man cut him off.

'Time for speaking is over. Now just listen. One, we don't want you people in our state at all. But if you are still coming, then you have to respect our culture. This is not UP or Bihar. Understand? This is MAHARASHTRA! Jai—'

And the rest of the gang said, 'Maharashtra!'

Then the men exited the shop and glared at the onlookers. One man's eyes locked with Udayan and he felt a shiver go down his body. There was pure hatred in the man's eyes. For a second, Udayan felt like the man had found out he was Bihari too. He wondered if the gang would turn on him. Fear pulsed through him. He instinctively began backing away. Thankfully, the man kept moving. They got on their bikes and thundered away, leaving Shankar seated on the pavement with his head in his hands.

*

Up until now, Udayan's life could have been described as idyllic—cynics might even use the word 'privileged'. His father worked a job where his collar was excessively white, his mother stayed at home and catered to his every need and they lived in a building where kids played hide-and-seek instead of *lukka-chhuppi*. In his brief eighteen years on Earth, not once had he encountered such vitriolic violence.

In the taxi ride home, he couldn't shake off the malice he had seen in the man's eyes. The sound of shattering glass and the animal cries of the men rang in his ears. He thought of Shankar. He had always liked the wiry juice-wallah. Shankar had always been nice to the students. He asked about their exams and sometimes even gave them a discount if they asked long enough. Seeing the helplessness in Shankar's face haunted Udayan.

At home, he spoke to no one. He skulked to his room and shut the door behind him. He opened his laptop and searched for the Maharashtra Pragati Party.

He learnt that the party had been formed a mere three years ago. Their symbol was a pair of scissors. A string of news articles showed that what had happened outside the college that day was not a stray incident. In fact, it was part of a strategy of intimidation that had been promised by the party leader, Manohar Deshpande. The leader was fifty years old. He had a square face, sharp nose and dark beady eyes that sat underneath furrowed brows. Udayan couldn't believe that a person could look so angry. It was as if this man had never smiled in his entire life.

Manohar Deshpande strongly felt that Maharashtra was being held back by outsiders. He used the word 'outsiders' when he was being polite. At most times, he would outright let people know that it was specifically the Biharis who were the scourge of his great state. He said that the Biharis were flooding the state, working for less money and stealing jobs. It was causing imbalance in society. Maharashtrians could not be sidelined in their own state, said Deshpande. Which is why he and his men had decided to take matters into their own hands to reinstate Marathi pride and let the Biharis know that they were not welcome.

In an oft-quoted line, Deshpande had summed it up by saying, 'We are using violence, but it is necessary. If someone breaks into your home, you don't say "Athithi Devo Bhava".'

The more he read, the more uneasy Udayan got. He realized just how close he had been to being a victim himself. Thank God those men in orange T-shirts hadn't figured out who he was. He would've been torn apart and the crowd around him would have silently looked on. They would have stared with vacant eyes, completely mute and accepting of every horror as long as it wasn't happening to them. Merely thinking about it made his insides twist into knots.

Just then the door opened, causing a startled Udayan into slamming his laptop shut. His mother strode in with lemon juice in her hand and concern on her face.

'Beta, are you feeling fine? You've not met us all day. What were you watching?' asked his mother.

Udayan thought about all the things he could say to explain his furtive behaviour and finally settled with 'Nothing.'

*

Udayan sat in a rickshaw with Aditi and her rotund, orange cat Laddoo, trying to determine which was howling more: the wind or Laddoo. The cat sat in a carrier on Aditi's lap. It was so large that Udayan wondered how Aditi had even managed to stuff it into the carrier.

They were taking Laddoo to the vet because the cat had thrown up four times over the course of one night. Being the pampered cat that she was, Laddoo had made sure to puke on four different spots of the same expensive carpet. She was discovered in the morning, feebly meowing in the middle of the carpet, leading to Udayan getting a frantic call from Aditi.

Now, they were hurtling across town with Aditi anxiously goading the rickshaw-wallah to drive faster and faster. Udayan was worried. The rickshaw was already trembling with the speed, if they accelerated any more, Udayan feared the rickshaw would explode. But he held on and hoped for the best.

They came to a signal and to Udayan's relief the rickshaw slowed to a halt. Beside him Aditi rocked back and forth. He saw her clasp and unclasp her fingers. Her feet shook impatiently.

'It's taking too long,' said Aditi.

Udayan knew that she loved that fat, orange sentient cushion. He had never asked her whom she loved more between him and the cat because he feared she would choose the cat. Now he could see the pain contorting her beautiful face. He couldn't bear to see her this way. He was compelled to do something that would put her at ease.

He leaned across to the driver and said, 'Bhaisahab, break the signal. It's an emergency. This cat needs a doctor.'

The driver looked in the rearview mirror and saw the grief-stricken Aditi and heard the mournful cries of Laddoo. He understood the situation clearly.

'Sir, the signal is red,' he said.

'I know. Break it. I need you to drive like an ambulance,' said Udayan.

'If we get caught, you will pay the fine?'

'Yes. Just go.'

He felt her fingers squeeze his arm. The rickshaw-wallah gunned the rickshaw and they broke the signal.

As they got to the other side, two traffic cops leapt out from the side of the road and with a firm outstretched hand, they commanded the rickshaw to stop.

The rickshaw-wallah glowered at Udayan in the rearview mirror.

The traffic cops prowled over to the vehicle. Their white uniforms were blinding in the afternoon light.

'License,' barked one of the cops.

'Sir, sorry,' bleated the rickshaw-wallah.

'Shut up!' said the other cop.

The rickshaw-wallah feel silent. He quietly got out of the vehicle, fished out his license and handed it over to the cops.

'Yadav?' said the cop, 'From Bihar?'

'Yes, sir.'

'See this', said the first cop to the other. 'This is the problem with these people. If you don't know how to follow the rules, why do you come here?'

Udayan's heart started pounding faster. He could feel the humiliation that was burning through the rickshaw-wallah's face. He could hear the slight shift in the tone of the cops. There was a superiority in the man's voice that stung him.

'Sir, it's not like that. The customer requested . . . they were in a hurry . . . that is why I jumped the signal.'

'The customer will ask you to kidnap someone, you'll do that also?' said one cop.

'He's Bihari. He might actually do it,' said the other.

The rickshaw-wallah turned to Udayan. 'Sir, say something.'

Udayan was frozen. His tongue felt like a paperweight in his mouth. His teeth were clenched. He looked from one cop to the other. They seemed to grow in size the longer he looked.

Just then Laddoo let out one of her trademark irritated shrieks. Everyone jumped. Aditi huffed in anger.

'Get out,' she said, nudging Udayan in the ribs.

Udayan squeaked out of the rickshaw. Aditi got out delicately, trying not to upset the already agitated Laddoo. She strode with the carrier to the cops and in chaste Marathi said, 'Sir, my cat is very ill. We need to get her to a doctor. It is an emergency. We are sorry we had to break the law, but this cat's life depended on it. Please let us go.'

And right on cue, Laddoo let out a howl that underlined the credibility of the story.

'Arre, you should have said this before,' said one cop.

'It's a very pretty cat,' said the other.

'But a law has been broken . . .' said the first cop.

'And there are penalties . . .' said the other.

Aditi walked back to Udayan and asked him for a 100-rupee note. She gave that to the rickshaw-wallah who slipped it into his license and handed it to the cops.

'Get well soon,' said the cop to Laddoo as Aditi got back into the rickshaw.

The driver took his seat and they got back on the road.

'Madam, if you weren't there, they would have taken a full week's earning,' said the driver.

'Perks of being a Maharashtrian,' said Aditi Chitre and went back to consoling the distraught Laddoo.

*

Udayan sat on a bar stool later that evening, studiously scribbling jokes into his notebook. He had found that he always got his best ideas right before an open mic began. Udayan had found his way to the stand-up comedy scene, the way a lot of people like him had—by people telling him, 'Hey, you're funny! You should try stand-up'. It had only been a few months since he had started going up on stage, but he loved it. On stage, he had the freedom to fully inhabit his being. He didn't have to censor himself for the people around him, he didn't have to think twice about blurting out the pinging thoughts in his mind and instead of being told to behave himself, on stage, his inherent silliness was encouraged. When he had the mic in his hand, time slowed down. The chatter in his mind dissolved into the singular monologue of his performance. He was always right there in the moment as long as he was on stage and the second he got off, he was pulled back into the chaotic stream of distraction and doubt.

Udayan usually liked performing at The High Tide Bar and Kitchen, a cosy, dimly lit bar at Versova. He had always gotten a better response there than at the other venues in the city. But today, he didn't feel at ease. He was going to be the third to perform and while he usually felt eager to go up, he wished he was lower on the list tonight. There were a lot of new faces amongst the comics in the line-up and he didn't feel like talking to them. He sat in silence, notebook in hand, staring at the faces in the crowd until he heard the host say his name.

Bundling up his nerves, Udayan climbed on stage, shook hands with the host and took hold of the mic. He smiled feebly at the audience.

'Hi . . .' he said, 'My name is Udayan . . .' he trailed off. He hadn't given his surname to the host and he wondered if he should say it out loud to the audience now. If he said it, they would identify him. They would know everything about him, dating back to a few centuries. They would label him and classify him. Just like Siddharth had been able to do. They would know he was an outsider.

He stared at the crowd. There were expectant faces in the crowd, faces that were keen to laugh and they hoped that this long pause was part of his act. They waited for a punchline they couldn't see coming. But even their anticipation seemed like aggression to Udayan. He could feel the expectation in the air. They wanted him to speak. But he couldn't. He felt paralysed just as he had been in front of the traffic cops. All his rehearsed lines, his practised witticisms, had deserted him suddenly. His mind felt vacant. His tongue seemed beyond his command. Time elongated. He felt vulnerable, hunted by eyeballs that were shrouded in darkness.

'I'm sorry . . .' he mumbled and got off stage.

There was silence for a few unending seconds. Then someone in the audience clicked his tongue. The host threw him a look, half-sympathetic, half-annoyed as he rushed past him to fill the vacuum on stage.

'All right, give it up for the shortest act of the night. Moving on . . .'

Udayan left with his chin tucked into his chest. He couldn't get himself to stand in the spotlight and talk into a microphone when all he wanted was to disappear.

*

It had been a rough week. Since the incident at the open mic, Udayan had not felt like himself. A thin-lipped anxiety had taken up a permanent position on his face. His conversations with Aditi had become monosyllabic. She tried to pry him open repeatedly, but he couldn't get himself to voice his fears. He couldn't tell his Maharashtrian girlfriend that he felt afraid around Maharashtrian people.

His parents' concern grew with his downbeat behavior. Every time he left a plate half-eaten, tears welled up in his mother's eyes. His father couldn't believe that he had let a whole weekend go by without hijacking the TV to watch a single football match. They tried every trick in the parent's interrogation handbook, even going as far as to say, 'You can tell us anything. Think of us as your friends.' And when that hadn't worked, they realized there was only one thing left to be done. He had to be taken to the oracle: Daadi.

Udayan shared a wonderful bond with his daadi. They shared almost no interests in common, owing to her being born several decades before him and not making much of an effort to keep up with the times. And yet they never ran out of things to talk about. It was because, ever since he could remember, Daadi had always spoken to him as an equal. She was never condescending or patronizing. Whatever childish inanity he could have spouted, she always considered it with the same thoughtfulness that she reserved for passages from the Ramayana. She was his confidant and his parents were counting on her to solve the riddle of his drooping temperament.

They arrived at Daadi's house a little after lunchtime. A familiar smell of garam masala and bhindi hung in the air. Her house was neat and orderly and stuck somewhere in the mid-80s, which is when Daadi had decided she was no longer going to keep up with trends. It was a warm reunion. They sat and chatted. Then on cue, Udayan's parents remembered errands they had to run and hurried out of the house.

Daadi settled into her recliner. On a table beside her were a neat stack of newspapers. She gently put on her bifocals and threw a sharp glance at Udayan.

'Why are you sad, Udu?' she asked.

'I'm not.'

Daadi waved her hand.

'The corners of your lips are touching the floor. What happened?'

Udayan remained silent.

'Is it a girl?'

Udayan shook his head. Daadi grew slightly concerned. Sadness in boys his age was common, but it not being about a girl was rare.

'I was just reading about a new drug called 'Heebie-Jeebies' becoming popular with college kids—'

'It's not drugs, Daadi.'

'All right then, don't tell me. I'm going to make some tea for the two of us and then we can talk about something else.'

She heaved herself out of the recliner and scuttled to the kitchen. Udayan heard pots clanging, a stove flaming to life and soon he was hit by the smell of tea and ginger. It was comforting. He missed spending the summers with Daadi. He felt bad about rudely rebuffing her concerns. When she returned with the tea, he spoke.

'Why did we come here?'

'We were getting a good deal on the flat. Your father was friends with the builder—'

'Not the flat, Daadi. Why did we come to this state? Maharashtra.'

Daadi's eyes narrowed. It was a very odd question. She studied her grandson. There was confusion and anger resting on his face. Her eyes then fell on the stack of newspapers beside her. Half a headline caught her eye: *Regional Politics*, it said. 'Could it be . . .' she wondered.

'Has someone said something to you?' she asked.

Udayan shook his head. Daadi wondered how she should address the situation and then chose honesty as she always did.

'Is it because of the things being said on the news?'

Udayan nodded. Daadi smiled.

'It's a good question to ask: why did we come to this state? The simple answer: your grandfather got a job at the textile mill in Parel. That was back when the mills would puff out clouds of smoke and at 4 p.m. the sirens sang. That's why we packed our life into seven boxes and boarded a train in the middle of July to come here. But let me tell you the other answer.'

Daadi settled further into the recliner.

'We came here because every part of this country is our own. It was a difficult decision to make for many reasons. We had to leave our family in Bihar, we had to leave the air and water that was familiar to us, we had to adjust to a new life. All of those things weighed on us. What never bothered us was: would we be accepted anywhere else? You know why? Because north to south, east to west, everywhere between the borders of this country, we knew was our own.

I want you to know this, the country is your home and the states are like its rooms. Do you think twice before going from one room of your house to another?'

'No,' said Udayan.

'Neither did we. We came here so that we could give your father and chacha a better life and this city welcomed us. We came here not knowing a single person and within weeks we had made some of our closest friends. This city has every type of person you can think of. Our neighbours were Maharashtrians,

Gujaratis, Tamilians, Oriyas and Punjabis. Each of them helped us in a hundred different ways. Mrs Deshmukh would send food every Sunday. The Kharats would watch over the kids when I had to go shopping. The Mohantys and us would go to Marine Drive together.'

Daadi saw that Udayan was growing impatient.

'You understand what I'm saying? Good. Now let me tell you something else. Even then there were some who said we were "outsiders". Because there will also be those who will try to gain power by dividing people. They will say that you don't belong here. They will say this is not your home.

'These people will always be there. But you shouldn't fear them because they are always small in number. Most folks don't believe them. Most people are like our neighbours. They care for the people you are, not the place you are from.'

'But most people do care where you are from. Most people don't like Biharis. They look down on us. They think we're rickshaw drivers and labourers. They mock us and make fun of us,' said Udayan.

Daadi chuckled.

'There's nothing wrong with being rickshaw drivers and labourers. They're all people like your grandfather and me. And they're earning an honest living. They're here to find a better future. To hell with those who make fun of them.

You have no reason to be embarrassed no matter what anyone tells you. Every region in this country has as deep a history, as rich a culture, as every other region. So if anyone makes fun of your heritage, know that it's mostly down to ignorance. Tell them to open Wikimedia and read a little.'

'Wikipedia, Daadi.'

'See, you can be as condescending as the rest of them.'

Udayan smiled. He then considered something else.

'But Daadi . . . they're beating people up. They thrashed our juice-wallah in front of my eyes.'

'And what did you do?'

'Nothing . . . I was scared.'

'That's why it happens. The few get away with injustice because the many are too afraid to act. Next time something like this happens, speak up. Call the police. Do something. Udu, people will frighten you as much as you let them. Don't let them frighten you. You have done nothing wrong. You were born an Indian and you live in India, all other labels come after that. You understand?'

Daadi was a small lady; head to toe, she was not more than 5 feet tall. Age had shrunk her further. Yet, she wasn't weak. Her wrinkled face was set in determination. Her voice was unwavering. In contrast to her courage, Udayan saw his cowardice magnified.

He felt a wave of guilt pass through him and on its heels, a wave of relief. She radiated strength and it was infectious. He was so glad he had spoken to Daadi. Suddenly, he was not afraid. There was no need to be.

He got up to hug her. She patted his shoulder.

'More tea?' she asked.

*

'Do you want to break up?' asked Aditi. Her eyes were wide. She was searching his face for the answer.

'What?' Udayan sputtered.

Udayan and Aditi had met for a date by the sea. They were walking down the promenade. It was five in the evening, when the sun's diagonal rays lit up the sea in a dazzle of gold. It was a beautiful day that suddenly turned overcast for Udayan.

'Why would you say that?'

They stopped. He was hoping Aditi would burst into laughter, tell him she was joking. Instead, she stood silently, waiting for him to speak.

'Was it something I said? Something I did?'

'It's the opposite, Uday. It's because you're not talking, not doing anything. I'm worried.'

He directed her to a bench.

'Have you started seeing someone else?' Aditi asked.

'NO!'

'Then why have you been so quiet. Why won't you talk to me? You don't want to go out. Are you upset with me? It feels like it's been weeks since I last saw you smile.'

Udayan had been so caught up in his own fear and anxiety that he had not stopped to think how his behavior must have affected others. He hadn't communicated his worries to Aditi because he thought she would be offended. She was a Maharashtrian after all. But now, he felt stupid for not confiding in her earlier. No wonder the poor girl was so alarmed.

So he took a deep breath and told her everything that had happened. He told her about Shankar's juice stall being pillaged, how he had been afraid of the hatred that was brewing against Biharis, the open mic where he was afraid to say his name and the growing politicization of the clashes as elections drew nearer. Finally, he told her about meeting his grandmother and how speaking to her had given him courage.

'Oh God!' said Aditi, 'It's a such a serious thing and you didn't tell me.'

'I thought you wouldn't understand . . .'

'Or you thought I'd also thrash you for being Bihari.'

'Keep talking like this and the MPP will give you a ticket.'

She linked her arm with his. 'You don't have to worry. I will love you no matter who wins the elections.'

He smiled.

'Talking to Daadi really helped, you know', said Udayan. 'I've been feeling much better but . . .'

'What?'

'I still don't have the guts to get back on stage.'

'Why?'

'I can't tell you what it felt like on stage that night. It was intimidating facing that crowd. You know I don't get nervous, but that night I was shaking, Aditi.'

'You need to go back on stage. I promise you'll be fine.'

'Yeah, I know . . .'

They sat in silence and stared the waves hitting the rocks. Aditi knew that he was unconvinced. She could almost hear the wheels spinning in Udayan's mind.

'What did your daadi say? She said to speak up, no? So, get on stage and talk about what you're feeling right now.'

'And say what? What's funny about Biharis getting beaten up because a politician wants to win an election?'

'I don't know . . . but I'm sure you'll figure it out. I'll tell you what, I'll come with you for the next open mic. Promise me you'll get on stage. Say whatever you want, but you get on that stage.'

Udayan smiled.

'Is that a yes?'

'Yeah. But if I get beat up then you're paying the hospital bills.'

'Yeah yeah, and I'll pay for your ticket back to Bihar also.'

Udayan's eyes went wide.

'What?' said Aditi, 'I was joking.'

With his heart rate doubling, Udayan excitedly said, 'I know!'

*

Bass thumped through the walls of the loft at The High Tide Bar and Kitchen. Udayan's grip tightened on his notebook as they entered the room. Aditi ran a comforting hand over his back.

'Don't worry, you'll be great,' she said. She leaned in and kissed him on the cheek. 'All the best!'

She left him to take a seat with the other audience members and Udayan headed to the back of the room, where comics were made to wait their turn. Sweat filmed his palms. He was shuffling to a seat when he caught the eye of the host. It was the same comic from last time. The host gave him a wide grin.

'Glad you're back, man. Remember to keep your set shorter this time,' said the host.

Udayan gave a feeble smile. He was nervous about his material and the ribbing from the host only made it worse. He sat down, opened his notebook and went over his jokes one last time. He had rehearsed them all night in front of his mirror, but he was afraid he was going to forget everything as soon as he stepped foot on stage. He took a few deep breaths in a failed attempt to calm himself.

Soon, the last audience members had taken their seat. The lights dimmed, music played and then the host bounced up on stage. He greeted the audience, bantered with them, did some jokes and introduced the first act. There were only fifteen people in the audience, but because it was a tiny room, the laughter sounded thunderous.

This time, Udayan had chosen to go towards the end of the line-up. He hoped the extra time would help him settle his nerves, but it was having the opposite effect. His leg hadn't stopped shaking as he waited. He kept studying the audience members and to his dismay he noticed them lose interest as the night went on. He regretted not going up first and getting the ordeal over with. He began imagining scenarios where he was on stage and the bored, tired audience started heckling him. He began pacing the back of the room, hoping the motion would distract him.

Soon, the host came up to him and said, 'You're next. Be ready.'

He bounced up and down and expelled breath.

'Please welcome Udayan Sinha!' said the host.

Udayan almost ran up on stage. He shakily shook the host's hand and grabbed the microphone off the stand. Then he stood huffing on stage. He was out of breath. He stood swaying for a few seconds getting his bearings. He peered into the audience. Then suddenly in the front row he spotted a large man in an orange shirt. The man had his arms crossed and was glaring at him. Udayan's heart rate quickened.

'Go Udayan!' came a voice from the crowd. He squinted his eyes and saw Aditi in the second row. He could dimly make out the giant encouraging smile on her face. 'You can do this,' she mouthed. He nodded. Seeing her steadied him. *Let's do this*, he thought. Then he pulled the microphone closer and spoke.

'Hi!' he boomed. The audience was taken aback. They weren't expecting such an exuberant start from Udayan's jittery demeanor. Udayan plowed on.

'My name is Udayan Sinha and I'm from Bihar.' He paused. The audience tittered nervously. The man in the orange shirt stared, unblinking.

'I'm a Bihari, but my girlfriend is Maharashtrian. So I'm not in a relationship; I'm in an adventure sport.'

As soon as he finished the line, there was a pause of half a second and then the room exploded in laughter. The noise washed over Udayan. His face lit up. The tension in his body began reducing.

'We don't have fights in our relationship and if you've been following the news recently, you'll know why. In general, it's not a good time for any Bihari to piss off a Maharashtrian.'

The crowd roared. Udayan's back straightened.

'She told her parents that she was dating a Bihari and they said, "Okay, since you like him, we'll break only one of his legs."'

The laughter ricocheted off the walls. He could see the host at the back of the room. His shoulders were bouncing up and down with laughter.

'She then told her parents I wanted to become a comedian. And they said, "Chalo, at least he's not stealing our jobs." I asked her, "Do they not think Maharashtrians can do comedy?" She said, "No, they just don't think comedy is a job."'

There was laughter and then it turned into applause. Seeing a room full of people double up with laughter erased all the doubts he had struggled with for all these weeks. Udayan couldn't stop smiling. He saw the man in the orange shirt uncross his arms and guffaw loudly, slamming two meaty palms together. Bolstered by the response, Udayan turned to him.

'Sir, are you Maharashtrian?'

The man was stumped. He didn't expect to be questioned.

'Yes,' he said.

'Sir, don't worry. After the show, I'm taking the train back to Patna.'

The man relaxed as the crowd broke into another fit of laughter. Suddenly, his burly build didn't faze Udayan. He felt relaxed. He felt in control again. Just as he usually did when he was doing his antics in front of his college friends.

'Sir, that orange shirt is lovely. The only thing missing are the words: Maharashtra Pragati Party.'

Laughter and applause. Udayan felt exhilarated. All this while, Udayan had thought that jokes were a weapon to attack people he didn't like. But as we watched the audience looking at him expectantly that night, he realized that they could be a shield to defend himself. He turned to look at Aditi. She wasn't laughing. Her face beamed with pride. She squeezed her eyes shut in affection.

'You know,' he told the audience. 'Before I did the show, I was scared. My girlfriend was the person who said I should go ahead with it.'

'Aww' went someone from the audience.

'I said to her,' continued Udayan, 'If someone beats me up, will you pay the hospital bills? And she said . . .'

He looked at her and winked. There could be no space for shame if one was simply shameless.

About the Authors

Parvati Sharma has written two books for children, *The Story of Babur* and *Rattu & Poorie's Adventures in History: 1857*. She has also written for adults: *The Dead Camel and Other Stories of Love*; *Close to Home*, a novella; and *Jahangir: An Intimate Portrait of a Great Mughal*, a historical biography. Sharma lives in New Delhi, where she has studied English literature and Indian history, and worked as a travel writer, editor and journalist.

Neha Singh is a Mumbai-based children's author, theatre practitioner and women's rights activist. She has authored eight books for children, contributed to two anthologies and has written poems, prose and non-fiction in Hindi for various children's literary magazines. Her books have been nominated for several national and international literary awards and *I Need to Pee* won a commendation at the South Asia Book Awards (USA) in 2018. Neha also writes, acts and directs theatre productions while running her own theatre company, Rahi Theatre. Four short films she wrote and directed garnered critical acclaim. Neha spearheads a women's rights campaign called 'Why loiter?' that aims at reclaiming public spaces for women by the simple act of loitering in them. She was named one of hundred most influential women in the world by BBC in 2016 for this campaign. She blogs about it at whyloiter.blogspot.com.

A writer, child-rights activist and award-winning actor, **Nandana Dev Sen** has written six children's books (translated into more than fifteen languages globally), and starred in twenty international feature films. After studying literature at Harvard and filmmaking at USC, she worked as a book editor, a screenwriter, a translator, a first responder to teens in crisis and as Princess Jasmine at Disneyland. Nandana has represented UNICEF, NCPCR and RAHI in the fight to end child abuse and human trafficking. Winner of the Last Girl Champion Award, she has served on the jury of multiple child-rights commissions, global film festivals and international literary awards, including the DSC Prize. Nandana is Artist Ambassador for Save the Children India, and can be reached on Facebook, Instagram, and Twitter (at Nandana Dev Sen).

Nikhil Taneja (@tanejamainhoon) is a Mumbai-based writer, producer, storyteller, teacher, entrepreneur and youth mental health advocate, who clearly did not 'settle' for doing one thing, like the Tanejas before him. He's the co-founder and CEO of a socially conscious youth media organization called Yuvaa, is the festival creative director of the India Film Project and serves on the Global Advisory Board of The Bill & Melinda Gates Foundation's community, Goalkeepers. If you resonated with his essay, Nikhil is excited (yay!) for you to read his upcoming book *Be a Man, Yaar* that tries to take the toxic out of masculinity, to be published by Penguin Random House India in 2022.

Hannah Lalhlanpuii is currently pursuing her PhD degree in the Department of English, Mizoram University. Her area of interest includes postcolonial literature, insurgency literature and trauma studies. She has written several short stories and poems which have been published locally within the state. *When Blackbirds Fly*, published by Duckbill Books, is her debut novel.

Sonaksha Iyengar is an illustrator, graphic recorder and book designer. They use art to contribute to social justice movements and work with organizations defending human rights and the environment. They are currently dreaming and drawing about mental health, community care, fat liberation, queerness and intersectional feminism. Find their work here: www.sonaksha.com or connect with them on Instagram @sonaksha and Twitter @sonakshaiyengar. Their pronouns are they/she.

Saina Nehwal is an Indian professional badminton singles player. A former world no. 1, she has won over twenty-four international titles, which includes eleven Superseries titles. Although she reached the world's

2nd in the 2009, it was only in 2015 that she was able to attain the world no. 1 ranking, thereby becoming the only female player from India and overall the second Indian player—after Prakash Padukone—to achieve this feat. She has represented India three times in the Olympics, winning a bronze medal in her second appearance. She is a recipient of the Rajiv Gandhi Khel Ratna award and the Padma Bhushan.

Japleen Pasricha smashes the patriarchy for a living! She is the founder-CEO and editor-in-chief of Feminism in India (FII), an award-winning digital intersectional feminist and bilingual media platform. She is also a TEDx speaker and was recognized as a Young Innovator in 2018 by World Summit Awards. She has represented FII at various international platforms like UN CSW, Rights Con, IGF, Amnesty Int, UN HRC and Stockholm Internet Forum, to name a few. She was featured by the German Ministry for Economic Cooperation and Development in a book on 'Women in Tech' for her work at FII and facilitated by Maneka Gandhi and the Ministry of Women and Child Development, GoI as Web Wonder Woman. She has also been recognized by the Swedish foreign minister for her work on the gender gap on Wikipedia. Currently, Japleen oversees the strategic vision and growth at FII.

She likes to garden, travel, hike, swim and cycle and is slowly moving towards a sustainable lifestyle.

Jane De Suza's writing is seriously funny. She has written books shortlisted for awards, stories translated across languages and for online games and film scripts. Her books include *Flyaway Boy*, *When the World Went Dark*, the SuperZero series, *Uncool*, *Happily Never After and The Spy who lost her Head*, among others. She is a management graduate from XLRI, was a creative director across advertising agencies and is a columnist with a national daily. She currently lives in Singapore with her family.

Andaleeb Wajid is the author of twenty-seven published novels and she writes across different genres such as romance, YA and horror. Her horror novel *It Waits* was shortlisted at Mami Word to Screen 2017 and her Young Adult series, The Tamanna Trilogy has been optioned for screen by a reputed production house. Andaleeb's novel *When She Went Away* was shortlisted for The Hindu Young World Prize in 2017. Andaleeb is a hybrid author who has self-published more than ten novels in the past two years.

Growing up in a bookstore, books taught **Anusha Misra** ways of dissent and how to take the road less travelled by. She is a psychology graduate from Lady Shriram College For Women, a writer and editor-in-chief of Revival Disability Magazine, a magazine on disability, sexuality and intersectional ableism. It is a magazine and an affirmative community of queer and disabled folks. Her writings are centred around the theme of disabled women occupying spaces, both mainstream and interpersonal. She is a columnist at various publications.

She describes herself as 'queer, chaotic and disabled' and strongly believes that intersectionality gives marginalized folks the emotional skin to survive in the world.

Kautuk Srivastava is a Mumbai-based writer, comedian and mammal. As a screenwriter, he has written many successful TV and web-based shows, including *MTV Reality Stars*, *Sumit Sambhal Lega* and *Shaitaan Haveli*. As a comedian, he's toured extensively across the country. He's part of the popular podcast, 'The Internet Said So' and his previous stand-up special, *Anatomy of Awkward*, is featured on Amazon Prime Video. His novel *Red Card* came out in 2018 and he's yet to shut up about it.